YOU ARE

FIGHTING FANTASY

THE HERO

THE
ITADEL
OF CHAOS

Fighting Fantasy: dare you play them all?

1. The Warlock of Firetop Mountain
2. City of Thieves
3. The Citadel of Chaos
4. The Forest of Doom
5. House of Hell
6. The Port of Peril

THE
CITADEL
OF CHAOS

STEVE JACKSON

 SCHOLASTIC

N

ICEFINGER

CHIANG
MAI

Kaad PAGAN

RED RIVER

Dark
Tower   Mirewater

DOGFISH
ISLAND   Flax CATFISH

ALLANSIA   PORT
BLACKSAND

WHITE

FIRE   OYSTER
ISLAND   BAY

SKULL COAST   SOUTHERN

BLOOD   THE DESERT OF
ISLAND   SKULLS

MOUNTAINS

Fang River KOK

Zengis

PLAINS

Anvil
Stonebridge Firetop
Mountain

KAY-PONG

DARKWOOD
FOREST
Yaztromo's
Tower

MOONSTONE
HILLS

RIVER

Largo

Deedle
Water

FOREST OF
SPIDERS

SILVER RIVER CHALICE

SILVERTON

Coven

KNOTOAK
WOOD

TROLLTOOTH
PASS

WATER RIVER

WINDWARD

FOREST
OF YORE

PLAIN

VALE OF
WILLOW

SALAMONS

TO THE
FLATLANDS

PLAIN

SHAZÂAR

Vatos

Black
Tower

CRAGGEN
HEIGHTS

LEO HARTAS

Scholastic Children's Books
An imprint of Scholastic Ltd
Euston House, 24 Eversholt Street, London, NW1 1DB, UK
Registered office: Westfield Road, Southam, Warwickshire, CV47 0RA
SCHOLASTIC and associated logos are trademarks and/or
registered trademarks of Scholastic Inc.

First published in the UK by Penguin Group, 1983
This edition published in the UK by Scholastic Ltd, 2017

Text copyright © Steve Jackson, 1983
Cover illustration copyright © Robert Ball, 2017
Inside illustrations copyright © Vlado Krizan, 2017
Map illustration copyright © Leo Hartas, 2017

The rights of Steve Jackson, Robert Ball and Vlado Krizan to be identified
as the author and illustrator of this work has been asserted by them.

Fighting Fantasy is a trademark owned by Steve Jackson
and Ian Livingstone, all rights reserved

ISBN 978 1407 18125 7

A CIP catalogue record for this book
is available from the British Library.

Printed by CPI Group (UK) Ltd, Croydon, CR0 4YY
Papers used by Scholastic Children's Books are made
from wood grown in sustainable forests.

1 3 5 7 9 10 8 6 4 2

This is a work of fiction. Names, characters, places, incidents
and dialogues are products of the author's imagination or are used
fictitiously. Any resemblance to actual people, living or dead,
events or locales is entirely coincidental.

www.scholastic.co.uk

CONTENTS

HOW WILL YOU START YOUR ADVENTURE?

The book you hold in your hands is a gateway to another world – a world of dark magic, terrifying monsters, brooding castles, treacherous dungeons and untold danger, where a noble few defend against the myriad schemes of the forces of evil. Welcome to the world of **FIGHTING FANTASY!**

You are about to embark upon a thrilling fantasy adventure in which **YOU** are the hero! **YOU** decide which route to take, which dangers to risk and which creatures to fight. But be warned – it will also be **YOU** who has to live or die by the consequences of your actions.

Take heed, for success is by no means certain, and you may well fail in your mission on your first attempt. But have no fear, for with experience, skill and luck, each new attempt should bring you a step closer to your ultimate goal.

Prepare yourself, for when you turn the page you will enter an exciting, perilous **FIGHTING FANTASY** adventure where every choice is yours to make, an adventure in which **YOU ARE THE HERO!**

How would you like to begin your adventure?

IF YOU ARE NEW TO FIGHTING FANTASY...

It's a good idea to read through the rules which appear on pages 224-232 before you start.

IF YOU HAVE PLAYED FIGHTING FANTASY BEFORE...

Make sure you've read the special rules concerning Magic on pages 230-235, and don't forget to enter your character's details on the Adventure Sheet which appears on page 236.

ALTERNATIVE DICE

If you do not have a pair of dice handy, dice rolls are printed throughout the book at the bottom of the pages. Flicking rapidly through the book and stopping on a page will give you a random dice roll. If you need to 'roll' only one die, read only the first printed die; if two, total the two dice symbols.

BACKGROUND

The lawful goodfolk of the Vale of Willow have lived for some eight years in awe and fear of the demi-sorcerer Balthus Dire. In awe – since his power is truly awesome – and in fear ever since word leaked from his domain that his ambitious plans of conquest were to commence with the Vale itself.

A faithful half-elf sent on a spying mission to the Black Tower came galloping back to the Vale three days ago with a frantic warning. From within the caverns of Craggen Rock, Balthus Dire had recruited an army of Chaotics and was preparing them to attack the Vale within the week.

The good King Salamon was a man of action. Messengers were sent throughout the Vale that day to prepare defences and to summon the menfolk to action. Riders had also been sent to the Great Forest of Yore to warn the half-elves that lived there and to make an appeal for allied forces. King Salamon was also a wise man. He knew well that the news would inevitably reach the Grand Wizard of Yore, a white sorcerer of great power, who lived deep within the forest. The wizard was old, and would not last through a battle of this magnitude. But he schooled a number of young magicians, and perhaps one of his students in the magic arts with courage and ambition would aid the king and his subjects...

You are the star pupil of the Grand Wizard of Yore. He has been a difficult Master and your own impatience has often got the better of you. Perhaps a little too headstrong, you left immediately for Salamon's court. The king welcomed you enthusiastically and explained his plan. The battle could be avoided without bloodshed if Balthus were to be assassinated before his army could be amassed.

The mission ahead of you is extremely perilous. Balthus Dire is surrounded, in his Citadel, by a multitude of appalling creatures. Although Magic is your strongest weapon, there will be times when you must rely on your sword to survive.

King Salamon has briefed you on your mission and warned you of the dangers that lie ahead. One way through the Citadel is the best for you to take. If you discover it, you will be successful with a minimum of personal risk. It may take you several trips to find the easiest way through.

You leave the Vale of Willow on the long hike to the Black Tower. At the foot of the hill of Craggen Rock, you can see its outline against the dark sky...

YOUR ADVENTURE AWAITS!

MAY YOUR STAMINA NEVER FAIL!

NOW TURN OVER...

*You hear muffled gruntings as you approach
and two misshapen creatures step forward*

The sun sets. As twilight turns to darkness you start your climb up the hill towards that forbidding shape silhouetted against the night sky. The Citadel is less than an hour's climb.

Some distance from its walls you stop to rest – a mistake, as it seems a fearful spectre from which there is no escape. The hairs on your neck prickle as you look towards it.

But you are ashamed of your fears. With grim resolve you march onwards towards the main gate, where you know guards will be waiting. You consider your options. You have already thought about claiming to be a herbalist, come to treat a guard with a fever. You could pose as a trader or an artisan – perhaps a carpenter. You could even be a nomad, seeking shelter for the night.

As you ponder the possibilities, and the yarns you will have to spin to the guards, you reach the main trail leading up to the gates. Two lanterns burn on either side of the portcullis.

You hear muffled gruntings as you approach, and two misshapen creatures step forward. On the left stands an ugly creature with the head of a dog and the body of a great ape, flexing its powerful arms. Its opposite number is indeed its opposite, with the head of an ape on the body of a large dog. This latter guard approaches you on all fours. It stops some metres in front of you, raises itself on its hind legs and addresses you.

Which story will you opt for?

Will you pose as a herbalist?   Turn to **261**

Will you claim to be
a tradesman?   Turn to **230**

Will you ask for shelter
for the night?   Turn to **20**

A little way up the passage there is a doorway on the right-hand side. This door has some strange scrawlings on it, but they are in a language that you do not understand. Will you try opening the door (turn to **142**), or will you continue up the passage (turn to **343**)?

3

What will you offer them:

A Pocket Myriad?	Turn to **327**
A Spider in a Jar?	Turn to **59**
A handful of Small Berries?	Turn to **236**

If you cannot offer any of these, you can either draw your sword (turn to **286**) or head for the far door (turn to **366**).

4

You conjure up a fireball and send it flying at the creature's face. You watch in dismay as it bounces off with no effect! You may either cast a quick Creature Copy Spell (turn to **190**), or draw your sword (turn to **303**).

5

You try the handle of the door and it turns, opening into another hallway. Some distance along, the passageway turns to the right and ends shortly in another door. On this door is a sign, which reads 'Please Ring for Butler'. A rope – evidently the bell – hangs by the door. Will you ring as instructed (turn to **40**), or try the door handle (turn to **361**)?

6

The path runs alongside the river for several metres and then cuts back into the rock. You follow the path for some time. Turn to **367**.

7

The door is locked. You may try to break it down by charging it with your shoulder (turn to **268**), or you may cast a Strength Spell on yourself and try to wrench the door off its hinges (turn to **116**).

8

She watches in astonishment as an exact duplicate of herself appears between the two of you. She backs off a little and you instruct your creation to attack. But as they get close to one another, a strange thing happens. They seem unable to get close to one another, like two spinning tops, and keep bouncing apart. But your own copy has at least forced the creature back some distance away from you, allowing you to run to the Citadel's main entrance. Turn to **218**.

9

Under your Illusion Spell, the crowd of onlookers see you start playing the game. You watch for a couple of rounds and the tension mounts. You decide it prudent to leave the room without wasting more time. Turn to **31**.

10

You feel around in the rock and eventually find a small lever. As you pull this lever, the rock face crumbles slightly and a narrow opening appears. You climb through this opening and find yourself in a passageway. Down the passageway to the left you can see a door and decide to investigate. Turn to **249**.

11

You may use either:

A Fool's Gold Spell	Turn to **36**
A Creature Copy Spell	Turn to **262**
An E.S.P. Spell	Turn to **128**
A Weakness Spell	Turn to **152**

If you have none of these, you will have to draw your sword and fight (turn to **16**).

Three ugly old women with long noses and chins are scooting around the room

12

He stands in front of you breathing heavily. His Spell was evidently quite exhausting. You may use this as an opportunity to:

Nip over to the armoury
cupboard   Turn to **274**
Spring under the table   Turn to **335**
Rush to the window   Turn to **78**

13

The handle turns and you open the door into another room, where there is plenty of activity. Three ugly old women with long noses and chins are scooting around the room – which seems to be a kitchen of some sort – taking various ingredients from the cupboards and adding them to a broth in a large kettle. There is a joint of meat roasting on a spit under a large chimney. As you look more carefully you can tell that the meat is not, in fact, an animal, but a whole Dwarf, turning black in the fire. One of the women glances at you and says, 'Ah, you must be the new servant ... or are you the next meal?' whereupon they all begin to cackle and shriek with laughter. Will you let them believe you *are* the new servant they are expecting (turn to **302**), or do you want to investigate the room further (turn to **215**)?

14

The shadow of the wall makes it very difficult to see. A loose stone slips and you lose your balance, teetering on the edge of what you realize must be a deep pit. *Test your Luck*. If you are Lucky, you regain your footing and step back to safety. You can then walk round the pit and continue (turn to **79**). If you are Unlucky, you fall in (turn to **100**).

15

The dagger is indeed a work of art and was undoubtedly worth a fair price. The blade is made of shiny metal and the hilt is a peculiar green leather, with inlaid stones. You read an inscription which tells you that it is an enchanted throwing dagger which never misses. In a future combat, you may use this dagger to throw at an opponent. It will automatically inflict 2 *STAMINA* points of damage without the need to roll for *Attack Strength*. But you may use it only once. You put the dagger into your belt and set off towards the Citadel. Turn to **245**.

16

Resolve your battle:

GARK   *SKILL 7*   *STAMINA 11*

After four *Attack Rounds,* you may *Escape* through one of the doors at the far end of the room (turn to **99**). If you wish to continue the battle, do so and turn to **180** if you win.

17

All manner of strange foodstuffs are in the cupboards. Eyeballs, tongues, small lizards, vials of liquids, herbs and berries of all different shapes and sizes. One particular bottle, of a translucent green liquid, catches your eye. You have no time to read the label there and then, so you put it quickly into your pocket while they are not looking. You tell them that their kitchen appears to be in order and leave through the door at the far end of the kitchen. Turn to **93**.

18

He points to a section just above the floor, which you peruse. Eventually you choose one volume and settle down to read through it. Balthus Dire is apparently third in a line of Sorcerer-Warlords ruling over the Black Tower and the Kingdom of Craggen Rock. He rose to power after the death of his father, Craggen Dire, some years ago. The Dires have been masters of Black Sorcery for generations, but their strength and power last during the nighttime only; sunlight is like a poison to them. Shortly after his father's death, Balthus Dire married the Lady Lucretia, herself a Black Sorceress, and since that time they have ruled together over the Kingdom of Craggen Rock. As you finish the book, you notice that the librarian is holding his hand to his ear, apparently listening to something. He glances up at you, quizzically. You may either look for another useful book which may aid you on your quest (turn to **84**), or attempt to leave the library through the door behind him (turn to **31**).

19

The staircase creaks as your foot falls on it. You try to ascend as quietly as possible, but the old timbers groan under your weight. Suddenly one of the stairs clicks as if to trigger a switch of some kind. To your surprise, all of the stairs flick downwards! You are now standing on a smooth, steep slope! Try as you might, you cannot keep your balance and you fall down the slope, tumbling head-over-heels. If you wish to use a Levitation Spell, you may fly up and out of danger, to land on the balcony above (turn to **363**); otherwise turn to **254**.

20

The Ape-Dog tells you that no one is allowed into the Black Tower after dark – you will have to look elsewhere for shelter. You may either resign yourself to a fight (turn to **288**). Or you may pick up a stone and cast a Fool's Gold Spell on it, offering them a nugget of gold as a bribe to let you in (turn to **96**). Deduct the Fool's Gold Spell from your Spells if you use it.

21

'What brings you to these parts?' she demands. You tell her your story, carefully avoiding telling her of your real mission. She advises that if you know any magic, you should flee from this place. The creatures you have met so far do not compare with those you will come across within the Citadel Tower itself. She tells you you will never meet the master without finding the Fleece first, and bids you luck on your mission. Add 2 *LUCK* points for the information you have learned and set off onwards. Turn to **6**.

22

You open the door and step out into a long, dark corridor. Turn to **188**.

23

You open the door and step out into a passageway which continues straight onwards for some time. It swings to the left, then back to the right, until you can see an archway ahead that opens out into a large room. You head forwards into the room. Turn to **169**.

24

You taste the wine and, as you are considering its flavour, you hear a clinking noise. You turn to look in the direction that the noise is coming from and you are horrified to see that the bottles in the racks are moving on their own. One bottle flies from its place and hurtles towards you, narrowly missing your head and smashing on the wall behind you. Another flies at you, then another, until you are being pelted by bottles from all directions. You realize that your only defence is to use a Shielding Spell. Cast this Spell if you can and turn to **372**. If you cannot cast this Spell, turn to **219**.

25

The door opens, allowing you into a large, circular room. You scratch your head quizzically. In the centre of the room you can see a small 'island', surrounded by a wide trench, on which stands a chest, locked with metal fastenings. The trench is too wide to jump and is very deep. Just inside the door is a length of rope. A door leads from the room, opposite the door you came in through. Will you:

Ignore the box and walk round the trench to the other door?	Turn to **206**
Cast a Strength Spell and leap across the trench?	Turn to **133**
Pick up the rope and formulate a plan?	Turn to **239**

26

Will you cast:

A Fire Spell?	Turn to **87**
A Weakness Spell?	Turn to **345**
A Creature Copy Spell?	Turn to **101**

If you have none of these, return to **304** and choose again.

27

As you hold out the Gold Pieces, the three creatures stop in their tracks. They gasp as they look at your coins. An invisible hand snatches them from you and lays them on the ground. They look at you and a voice demands more. You pull out *all* your Gold Pieces and throw them into the centre of the room. A voice rings out: 'Well, stranger, you are indeed welcome here in the house of the MIKS. We thank you for your gift. If you are heading on, take the door ahead of you, but beware of the Ganjees. We wish you luck with your journey.' You may add one *LUCK* point for the Miks' good wishes, and leave through the door ahead of you. Turn to **206**.

28

You cast the Spell and conjure up a ball of fire in your hands. They stop in their tracks and watch you carefully. You toss the ball towards them and they shriek in fright, rolling away in terror from your obvious powers. While you still have control over the Spell, you create three smaller fireballs and pitch one at each of them. They howl and scatter, rolling up the corridor away from you. You may now proceed up the left-hand passageway (turn to **243**), or up the right-hand passageway (turn to **2**).

29

Cautiously, you approach the little man. As you get close, a single eye opens and looks you straight in the face. A wide grin spreads between the creature's ears and he disappears! 'Good mornin' to yer!' says a chirpy little voice behind you, and you swivel round to see him standing there, still grinning. 'I'm O'Seamus, the Leprechaun!' he chuckles, and holds his hand out to you. He seems friendly enough – will you shake his hand and try to befriend him (turn to **271**), or draw your sword (turn to **131**)?

30

The beast is immensely powerful. You draw your sword and the battle starts:

CLAWBEAST   *SKILL 9*   *STAMINA 14*

When you have inflicted your fourth hit on the creature, turn to **241**.

31

You leave the games room through the door in the far end of the room, which opens into a short passageway ending at a large wooden door. The handle on this door turns, letting you into a large chamber. Turn to **169**.

32

Stepping over the bodies, you approach the gate and call for the gatekeeper, hiding in the shadows as he approaches. He sees the bodies and comes out to investigate, whereupon you nip inside the gate and lock him out. Turn to **251**.

33

As you try to rise, the Orc and the Goblin grab you and hold you down, while the Dwarf advances with his club. Turn to **213**.

34

The key turns and, removing the lock, you open the box to find another key, this time cut in a glowing green metal. Will you try this new key on the third box (turn to **89**) or leave the room with the two keys (turn to **237**)?

35

You concentrate on your Illusion. You can either convince him that he is being attacked by an enemy (turn to **364**), or make yourself disappear in the hope that he will come looking for you (turn to **246**).

36

'Pah!' says the Gark, 'I do not fool that easily. Throw your lumps of brass away.' It dawns on the creature that, if you are offering a bribe, you must be an intruder which – for a Gark – is quite a stunning piece of logical thinking! It slaps you hard with its great hand, knocking you unconscious onto the floor. The last words you hear before you pass out are the proud Gark's: 'Into the jail for this one!' Turn to **234**. And don't forget to deduct your wasted Fool's Gold Spell.

37

You draw out the skin and the creature hisses loudly. All its heads retreat and it remains still, watching you. There is a door on the far side of the room and you slowly make your way towards it. Halfway across the room, a head darts out and snatches the fleece from your hands. But instead of attacking you, the Hydra slinks back into a corner. You move on to the door cautiously. Turn to **229**.

38

The door opens into a short passageway which is paved with small stones. A short distance further on, an ornately carved door marks the end of the passageway. But just before the door, a side passage leads off to the left. You approach the door, listening for any signs of life inside. As your hand touches the handle, a voice says: 'Do not knock; just enter!' from inside. Will you enter the room as instructed (turn to **132**) or will you decide against this room and take the passage leading off to the left (turn to **306**)?

39

You take out the Jar and, as you do so, the Ganjees gasp. 'Racknee!' says a voice. 'You have returned!' And with those words, an invisible hand snatches the jar from you, lays it onto the ground and opens the lid. The Spider-Man turns towards you and growls a little growl. You draw your sword as the beast scuttles towards you angrily. You must fight the creature:

SPIDER-MAN   *SKILL 7*   *STAMINA 5*

As soon as the Spider-Man gets its first hit on you, turn to **208**. If you win without it wounding you, you must now face the Ganjees with your sword. Turn to **248**.

A hunchbacked, misshapen creature with rotten teeth, ragged hair and tattered clothes stands in front of you

40

After several moments the door opens slowly and a hunchbacked, misshapen creature with rotten teeth, ragged hair and tattered clothes stands in front of you. 'Yes, sir (heh, heh) – what can I do for you?' growls the half-human creature. 'I am expected,' you reply, and walk past him through the door with confidence. He is a little bewildered by your manner and stammers, not knowing whether to challenge you or not. 'Which way to the reception room?' you demand. He squints at you through one eye and motions towards a left fork in the passageway a short distance ahead. Will you believe him and take the left fork (turn to **243**), or do you distrust this shifty creature and take the right fork (turn to **2**)?

41

The three women shuffle together in a huddle and mutter under their breath to one another. With a little chuckle, one of them turns to you and says, 'Yes, stranger, we'll help you on your way.' She fixes you with ice-cold eyes, and points her finger first at you, then at the wall behind her. The room goes dark, you feel a rushing sensation and, when the darkness clears, you are in another room. Turn to **257**.

She blinks and the jets of fire disappear. What will you offer her?

A Silver Mirror?   Turn to **138**
A Hairbrush?   Turn to **91**
A Jar containing a Spider-Man?   Turn to **223**

If you have none of these, you must make some excuse about losing your gift and go back onto the balcony where you may take either the middle door (turn to **64**) or the far door (turn to **304**).

43

As you cast the spell, his grip loosens. Gradually his strength ebbs until eventually he releases his grip and slumps back, panting, on the ground. Lose 1 more *STAMINA* point as you nurse your wounded arm, and cross the Weakness Spell off your list. You can continue on your way. Turn to **14**.

44

The room stops shaking and you drop to the ground. The armoury cupboard is locked, but you may smash the lock. Or you may take off your backpack and look for a weapon to use. Which will you do:

Choose a weapon from
the cupboard?   Turn to **353**
Take an artefact from
your backpack?   Turn to **277**

45

If your stomach will bear it, you may try:

Some of the meat hanging up   Turn to **166**
A piece of fruit   Turn to **313**
A slice of cheese   Turn to **253**
A loaf of bread   Turn to **97**

46

With a motion, you fling your hand forward and point to the floor beneath the sorcerer. Smoke and flames burst from the ground. Balthus Dire jumps back a little, startled, then closes his eyes to concentrate. As they open, you can see a fire burning within the pupils themselves, and he steps forward into the flame you created. Taking a handful of flaming rubble, he throws this at you. Will you duck to avoid it (turn to **195**), or jump out of the way (turn to **74**)?

47

What Spell will you use:

Creature Copy Spell?	Turn to **8**
Illusion Spell?	Turn to **173**
Levitation Spell?	Turn to **259**

If you have none of these spells, you will have to retreat towards the monument in the centre of the courtyard and hide from her (turn to **209**).

48

'Never!' screams the sorcerer, spinning round from the shadows to face you. This time it is you who feels the quake of fear as you see that he has also changed himself – but into a creature which may cause a Fire Demon to stop in its tracks. Balthus Dire's face has become ugly and witch-like and his hair now seethes and squirms with small, hissing snakes. Will you retreat from this creature (turn to **232**) or leap forward with your Trident (turn to **199**)?

49

The creature gazes at you quizzically as if it is uncertain about you. Turn to **255**.

50

Turn to **164**.

51

You slash about madly with your sword but cannot hit the creature. Either it is extremely quick, or it has no solid body for you to hit! Its teeth are now tearing at your flesh and you can feel blood on your leg. You will have to protect yourself with your magic, or face certain death from this unseen creature. Will you cast a Strength Spell (turn to **301**), a Weakness Spell (turn to **159**), or, if you cannot or will not cast either, turn to **280**.

52

The door opens and you stride onwards, slamming it shut behind you. A short distance ahead, you reach a three-way junction, where you take the northwards passage. This continues for several metres leading to another door. You can hear laughter and merriment on the other side. Cautiously you open the door into a large room where a party of a dozen or so creatures, of all shapes, sizes and colours, are playing games. As you step into the room, a voice shouts, 'Look, this must be Glaz-Doz-Fut!' whereupon they all welcome you, inviting you to join the fun. Evidently they are expecting someone and have mistaken you for their missing guest. Will you play along and join them (turn to **385**), or will you tell them they are mistaken and try to make your way over to the door on the other side of the room (turn to **227**)?

53

'What do I want with your berries?' she laughs. 'My appetite died with my body!' And as you look closer you can see that she too is nothing but a Ghost. She floats across in the air towards you. Turn to **194**.

54

You search through your backpack. What will you pull out:

A Jar of Ointment?   Turn to **287**
A Pocket Myriad?   Turn to **160**
Gold Pieces?   Turn to **27**

If you have none of these, you will have to return to **104** and choose again.

55

You follow the passageway for some time. It turns to the right and eventually reaches a dead end. You may either return to the fork and take the other passage (turn to **249**) or you may look for secret passages (turn to **10**).

56

The BLACK ELF approaching you is skinny and ragged. He asks whether you are a guest or an adventurer. You tell him you are a guest, come down to sample the wine he keeps in his famous Wine Cellar. With a certain pride, he shows you the vintage bottles he keeps for his Lord, the Demi-Sorcerer. Some of them, he claims, have magical powers. He offers to let you sample the wine. Will you try a sample of:

The Red Wine?	Turn to **120**
The White Wine?	Turn to **163**
The Rosé Wine?	Turn to **334**
Decline his offer and make your way onwards?	Turn to **95**

57

Test your Luck. If you are Lucky, turn to **150**. If you are Unlucky, turn to **233**.

58

As you enter, the Gremlins flutter and squeak excitedly, then fly past you, through the door and out into the night. You are now alone with the chalices. Will you risk taking a drink? If so, will you choose:

The clear liquid?	Turn to **298**
The red liquid?	Turn to **267**
The milky liquid?	Turn to **92**

Or will you leave and head for the Citadel (turn to **156**)?

59

They are revolted by your gift and run over to the corner of the room, hiding under the beds. Somewhat puzzled by their behaviour, you leave the Jar on the floor and make for the door on the far side of the room. Turn to **140**.

60

The creatures become suspicious as you press them for information. The Dwarf springs to his feet brandishing a wooden club, while the Goblin and the Orc grab swords and glare at you. The Goblin's mistress shrieks and steps back several paces as the others advance towards you. You will have to fight them. You may use a Magic Spell:

Levitation Spell	Turn to **33**
Illusion Spell	Turn to **295**

Or you may draw your sword and fight (turn to **213**).

61

You advance with your sword. The Devlin stops . . . then springs at you! You slash with your sword but cannot harm the creature, which is now on top of you. Its flaming body is burning your flesh and you are in agony. Still it holds on and you pass out in shock. You fall to the ground never to wake again as the Devlin makes sure that your body is scorched beyond recovery. You will, after all, be the next meal for the creatures of the Black Tower. . .

62

With the Gargoyle out of action, you decide to investigate the box in the creature's pedestal. *Test your Luck.* If you are Lucky, you may take the pouch of 10 Gold Pieces locked inside. If you are Unlucky, you do not manage to open the box. Leave the room by turning to **140**.

63

You turn to the index and look up the reference. Turning to the correct page, you are dismayed to find that the section has been ripped out of the book! You may either turn to the *Calacorms* (turn to **263**), or look up the *Miks* (turn to **135**).

Looking up at you quizzically are three small creatures

64

You listen at the door and can hear squeaky voices laughing and squabbling. You try the handle and the door opens. Inside is a brightly coloured room. A few small beds are in one corner, and strewn about the floor are small mannequins of various brutish creatures. Along the right-hand wall is a large box and just beyond the box is a door. In the centre of the floor, and looking up at you quizzically, are three small creatures. They are human-like but have green skin, pointed ears and slit-like eyes. What will your approach be? Will you:

Draw your sword and prepare
to fight them?   Turn to **286**
Look in your pack for something
to offer them?   Turn to **3**
Walk confidently across the
room to the far door?   Turn to **366**

65

You kneel before him and bow. He is indeed your master now. You have failed in your mission.

66

They look at each other and chatter. One steps forward and holds out a small cube which looks as though it has been made of some kind of bread or cake. At his request, you pop it into your mouth and chew it. As you swallow it, you feel suddenly strong again. Restore your *SKILL* and *STAMINA* scores to their *Initial* levels and add 1 *LUCK* point. You thank him for the food, thank them all for their company and head for the doors. Turn to **270**.

67

You begin your fight with the creature. Your first blow is lucky and severs one of its six heads. The other five strike at you and, to your horror, two more heads grow where the other one died! One of the heads bites deep into your arm. Lose 4 *STAMINA* points. Your sword is obviously going to be of little use. Will you use a Creature Copy Spell (turn to **143**) or something from your backpack (turn to **226**)?

68

'Which would I take, eh?' he muses. 'Let's see... I would not take the one two doors to the left of the copper-handled one, nor the door to the right of the bronze-handled one.' Which one will you choose:

The brass-handled door?	Turn to **207**
The copper-handled door?	Turn to **22**
The bronze-handled one?	Turn to **354**

69

The creature is not very talkative, but you do discover that you are in the dungeons beneath the Black Tower and you will probably never be released, unless you are given to the Ganjees for sport. When you question him about Balthus Dire, he goes silent. You had better try a Spell to get you out of this prison. Turn to **193**.

70

You fly up and away from his lunges but he stands his ground and there is no way for you to fly around him to the door. Eventually the Spell wears off and you must face him once again. Will you:

Use a Weakness Spell?	Turn to **307**
Use a Strength Spell?	Turn to **264**
Draw your sword?	Turn to **325**

71

You draw your sword and hack at the tentacle. The tentacle will not fight back as will a normal creature, but instead is trying to drag you into a large hole in the ground which is opening around its base. You do not need to roll for the tentacle, as it has an *Attack Strength* of 15 and a *STAMINA* score of 2. Throw for combat in the normal way, but if your own *Attack Strength* comes to less than 15, do not subtract any points from your own *STAMINA*. However, if you do not defeat the creature within 3 *Attack Rounds,* it succeeds in dragging you into its lair and your adventure is over. If you do defeat it, you can peel the tentacle off your leg and proceed to the main entrance to the Black Tower. Turn to **218**.

72

Luck is not with you. Your first glance at the serpent-headed creature was enough to seal your fate. You cry out in anguish as you feel your joints begin to seize and your limbs become heavy and uncontollable. As the Gorgon's stony stare takes effect, you fight for balance – but lose it and crash to the floor. Your petrified body cracks on impact and you now lie in several pieces before Balthus Dire.

You have failed in your mission.

73

Either you may try to cut yourself free from the Sewer Snake, or you may ward it off with a Spell. If you will fight the creature, resolve this battle:

SEWER SNAKE   *SKILL 6*   *STAMINA 7*

If you win, turn to **112**.

If you wish to cast a Strength Spell, add 3 to your dice roll on your *Attack Strength*. If you wish to cast a Fire Spell, turn to **282**.

74

As you jump to the side, the sorcerer's eyes follow you – and so does his fireball! It hits you in the chest, knocking you over. The scorching will cost you 4 *STAMINA* points. If you are still alive, you may prepare another Spell for your counter-attack. Turn to **377**.

75

You step through the doorway, close the door behind you and wait for some time. You hear the footsteps run closer and reach the door. Incomprehensible chatterings on the other side of the door eventually die down and again you hear footsteps, this time moving away from you. You ring for the butler. Turn to **40**.

76

While you were pulling out your Berries, Balthus Dire has been concentrating on a Spell. He looks up and bursts out laughing. 'Slumberberries!' he cries. 'And what are you expecting me to do? Pop them into my mouth?' He snaps his fingers and his Spell materializes. Turn to **191**.

77

Balthus Dire is surprised at your success. 'So!' he exclaims. 'You think yourself stronger than the rest, eh?' You may act quickly and cast a Spell at him. Which will you choose:

An E.S.P. Spell?	Turn to **187**
A Fire Spell?	Turn to **46**
A Creature Copy Spell?	Turn to **349**

If you have none of these, or would prefer not to cast a spell, turn to **355**.

78

His eyes follow you to the window. His pupils have turned milky white. He leans his head back, blinks once and moans. Snapping his head forwards, he now glares at you with eyes that have turned to shining silver! His gaze is hypnotic, and you will have to act quickly. Will you:

Hide yourself behind one of the drapes?	Turn to **324**
Pull one of the drapes down and throw it over his head?	Turn to **124**
Look through your backpack for something to use?	Turn to **277**

79

In the far corner of the courtyard, you come across a peculiar bush with branches twisting out from the central stalk, as if in agony. The leaves are diamond-shaped, with small berries underneath, flat and tablet-like. You may take some berries with you on your adventure and creep further along the wall to the main entrance to the Citadel. Turn to **218**.

80

As you leap across the table, the sorcerer spins round. You stumble and crash to the ground as you see that he has changed into a creature much more dangerous than you. His face is now that of a witch, and his hair is now a mass of snakes, writhing and hissing at you. Will you continue your attack (turn to **199**) or retreat from him (turn to **232**)?

81

The Ape-Dog laughs and tells you that Kylltrog is a lazy good-for-nothing and is not worth saving. You breathe a sigh of relief as he walks back and shouts for the gatekeeper. Moments later, the gatekeeper appears and opens a small doorway to let you in. Turn to **251**.

82

You fall into the trench. Frantically, you try to grasp the edge as you tumble over, but without success. Head over heels you tumble down the pit, and your last memory is your final crash as you hit the ground below, which kills you instantly.

You have failed in your mission.

83

The man is a merchant. You tell him you are of the same profession and you chat for some time about prices and profits within the Black Tower. He says he has never been allowed above the ground floor of the Citadel, as merchants are rather despised inside. You bid him farewell and press onwards. Turn to **245**.

84

As you study the shelves, you hear a commotion behind you. You wheel round in time to see Orc-like creatures, armed and on guard, materializing one after the other behind you. They advance and surround you. The tallest one moves his face close to yours and blows a puff of breath straight into your eyes. The room spins and you slump to the ground, unconscious. Turn to **234**.

85

You cast your Spell and wait for a fireball to appear on the end of your torch. The torch flickers, just enough for you to see that there is a door on the far side of the room, but then goes out again. The Ganjees laugh once more at your efforts to thwart them. You feel a blow on the head which knocks you to the ground again. Lose 2 *STAMINA* points. Will you:

Try an Illusion Spell?	Turn to **395**
Take something from your backpack?	Turn to **322**
Draw your sword?	Turn to **248**

86

As you cast the spell, the two creatures watch in amazement as you rise in the air, float over their heads towards the gate, over the wall and into the Citadel. You land on your feet inside the gate and look around. Turn to **251**. But beware! They will be sure to alert the Citadel guards. Cross the Levitation Spell you have just used off your *Adventure Sheet*.

87

You create a large fireball in your hands and throw it at the creature. It has no effect. The Gargoyle swipes at you and the blow knocks you off your feet.

Lose 2 *STAMINA* points. You had better avoid this beast by leaving the room and trying the middle door on the balcony. Turn to **64**.

88

The door is extremely strong, but cracks a little under your charge. You may try charging it as often as you wish until you break it. Roll a die for each attempt. If you roll a six, you succeed (turn to **292**). For each unsuccessful attempt, you must lose 1 *STAMINA* point. If you decide against this course of action, you may use a Strength Spell (turn to **170**), or try either the middle door (turn to **64**) or the door at the far end of the balcony (turn to **304**) instead.

89

The key turns, the lock clicks open and you look inside the box. Inside the box is a glass jar, and in this jar is a spider. But not a normal spider; this creature has the face of an old man. He is talking to you, but you cannot make out what he is saying. A noise startles you and you spin round to see that the door, the one you came through, is beginning to open. You put the jar in your bag and make for the other door. Turn to **237**.

90

The passageway widens and you are now walking alongside a flowing river. Just ahead, a woman seems to be washing clothes. She has a basket of these clothes beside her, and several sets of long johns are hanging on a line behind her. Will you:

Draw out your sword and advance ready for a fight?	Turn to **176**
Hail her and try to make conversation?	Turn to **21**
Use an E.S.P. Spell to find out who she is?	Turn to **329**

91

She looks at your offering and her eyes widen. 'Let me see that,' she commands. You carefully advance towards her and hold out the brush. She snatches it and spends several moments admiring it. 'This is indeed a work of art,' she says, and she gets out of bed to try it in front of her mirror. As she brushes her hair with it, her hair takes on an unusual sheen, glimmering softly. She is fascinated with your gift and now is your chance to leave unnoticed through a door in the far corner. You may try to take with you a Golden Fleece which is lying on the bed. *Test your Luck*. If you are Lucky, you manage to snatch it quickly and can leave through the other door (turn to **140**). If you are Unlucky, you may *Test your Luck* again until you are finally Lucky. Or, if Luck is not with you, you may ignore the cumbersome thing and leave anyway (turn to **140**).

92

The milky liquid smells sweet. You take a sip and start to giggle! You take a gulp and burst out laughing – for no reason at all! No wonder the little Gremlins were enjoying it so much. Light-headed, and in fine spirits, you leave the chamber to make your way onwards towards the Citadel. Turn to **156** and add 2 *STAMINA* points for this refreshing incident.

93

Outside the door you look at your bottle. It is a bottle of Hogweed Essence, apparently useful for repelling stone-based creatures. This may be useful and you put it carefully into your backpack. Heading on up the corridor, you come to another door, which opens, letting you pass into a large room. Turn to **169**.

94

You feel your own growing power. Running at the door you hit it hard with your shoulder . . . but it does not budge! Lose 1 *STAMINA* point for your bruise and knock loudly to summon the guard. Turn to **118**.

95

At the far end of the Wine Cellar is a wooden door, which you try. It opens out into a passageway which leads onwards for several metres. Turn to **367**.

96

They accept your offering and summon the gatekeeper, who opens a small doorway in the portcullis to let you in. You leave them squabbling over the gold nugget. Turn to **251**.

97

The bread is rather tasteless and dry. In fact it is very dry – so dry that you are soon desperate for a drink! Your mouth is parched and you frantically search through the food in the room for something to drink. But there is nothing to quench your thirst. You must deduct 1 *SKILL* point until you find liquid of some sort which you may drink (drinking this liquid need not necessarily be given as an option – it may just be described as being present in a room). You may how leave the room, either through the door in the left-hand wall (turn to **13**) or through the one opposite the door you entered through (turn to **281**)

98

The GOLEM advancing towards you is a slow-moving creature, and you reach the boxes easily. You curse as you find they are all locked. As you struggle with the locks, the Golem closes on you. You may:

Draw your sword and fight the creature	Turn to **303**
Cast a Fire Spell	Turn to **4**
Cast a Creature Copy Spell	Turn to **190**
Forget the boxes and race for the door	Turn to **237**

99

Will you take either the left-hand door (turn to **52**) or the right-hand door (turn to **38**)?

100

Do you have a Levitation Spell? If so, you had better use it now to float out of the pit. If you levitate yourself, you can continue down the wall towards the corner of the courtyard (turn to **79**). If not, turn to **276**.

101

A duplicate of the creature materializes between the two of you. At your command, the battle commences:

GARGOYLE   *SKILL 9*   *STAMINA 10*

If your creation wins, turn to **62**. If your created Gargoyle loses, you decide against facing the Gargoyle on your own and leave the room, trying the door in the middle of the balcony. Turn to **64**.

102

They sympathize with your request. Three of them turn

towards the other one and, with obvious reluctance, this one takes an amulet from around his neck. This,' he says, 'is a Charmed Amulet. It is made of metal but a Jewel of Light is set into it. Ganjees fear this talisman, but they will no doubt try to trick you into losing it. This has been my own proud possession for some time but we Scouts are obliged by our gods to offer help, so I give it to you.'

You thank him and place the Charmed Amulet around your neck. You may now leave the room, but you may feel obliged, because of his great gift, to give him something in return. If you have any Gold Pieces, decide how many you will give him, cross these off your list, and turn to **183**. If you have no gold but will give him an artefact you have picked up, cross this off your list and turn to **396**. If you cannot, or will not, give him a gift in return, turn to **270**.

103

You cast your Spell – but nothing happens! You fall down and down from the tower, finally landing with a fatal crash on the floor below. The fearsome creatures have robbed you of your magic, and now of your life.

You have failed in your mission.

You try the handle and it turns. The door is stiff and you must shove it open. The room inside is some sort of living abode, with tables, chairs, shelves and a collection of animal heads on the wall. There is a plush pile carpet on the floor. Suddenly, one of the animal heads turns and looks towards you. It is some kind of dog, and it barks loudly in a tone which is a warning, both to you and to any of its cronies which may be within earshot. As you watch the head, you do not notice a carpet, which flies up off the floor and whisks past you, clipping your ear. You spin round in time to see one of the chairs, slowly re-forming itself into a tall man. 'What business have you here?' he booms. Will you:

Try to talk with him?	Turn to **266**
Use one of your Spells?	Turn to **310**
Search through your backpack for a weapon or a gift?	Turn to **54**
Leave the room quickly and try the other door?	Turn to **25**

105

The wine is rather bitter and, as you savour it in your mouth, you feel a burning sensation. You spit the wine to the ground and, to your amazement, a jet of flame flies from your lips! You may take a sample of the wine with you and use it instead of casting a Fire Spell, whenever the Fire Spell option is given. Your sample will be enough for a single usage. You head onwards towards a door leading further into the cellar. Turn to **95**.

106

She laughs again and tells you she likes to see people getting angry. In good humour, she accompanies you for several metres. Conversation is difficult. She sees something in the distant shadows and nips off to investigate, allowing you to advance to the Citadel's main entrance. Turn to **218**.

107

You have caught either 1, 2, 3 or 4 heads in your noose. These heads struggle to free themselves, but the creature continues its advance. You begin to panic as you try to decide what to do next. Turn to **184**.

108

You grasp the rope firmly, step back, and take a run at the putrid river. Suddenly, the rope snatches and whips with a mind of its own! You quickly let go and drop down to the ground. The rope drops on top of you and tangles itself around you. You realize that it is not a rope but, in fact, a long SEWER SNAKE, which wraps itself around your body and neck. Turn to **73**.

109

The creature strains against the barrier of your Shielding Spell. To your horror, it is so strong that it actually breaks through! It is now on top of you and you must draw your sword. Turn to **30**.

110

Test your Luck. If you are Lucky, you choose another name which is familiar to them and they summon the gatekeeper, who eventually appears to let you in (turn to **251**). If you are Unlucky, this was another poor guess and they advance towards you with their weapons at the ready. You will have to fight them (turn to **288**).

111

You have managed to avert your eyes from the creature and you now back into the corner, shielding your face with your arm. But what can you do? If you have a Polished Silver Mirror, you may pull it out of your backpack and hold it towards the sorcerer (turn to **347**). If not, turn to **153**.

112

You disentangle yourself from the dead Sewer Snake and try crossing the water. You get across without any further incidents, but you are certainly looking forward to your next bath! You continue along the passageway until you reach a junction where you can either go straight on or take a passage off to the left. If you fork left, turn to **212**. If you wish to go straight on, turn to **367**.

113

You cast the Weakness Spell at the sorcerer. He stops in his tracks and looks at you. His expression changes to one of pain and his shoulders shudder. Some sort of terrible internal turmoil is taking place within him. Will you wait and see what happens (turn to **388**) or draw your sword and advance (turn to **145**)?

114

You point to the base of the tentacle and cast your spell. A puff of smoke and flash of light burst from the hole in the ground. A shudder runs through the tentacle and, thankfully, it releases its grip. As it retreats back into the ground, you rub your leg to get the circulation back and then set off towards the main entrance to the Citadel again. Remember to deduct your Fire Spell and turn to **218**.

115

Your situation is not good. Balthus Dire strides towards you and is almost upon you. Turn to **373**.

116

Your super-powered hands grip the handle and tug. It comes off in your grip. You bunch up a fist and slam it into the centre of the door. The wood cracks and breaks, allowing you to break through into the room beyond. Turn to **210**.

117

As you draw your weapon, the sorcerer does likewise. You are now too close for either of you to use magic and you will have to finish off your battle in the most difficult sword fight you have had. Turn to **337**

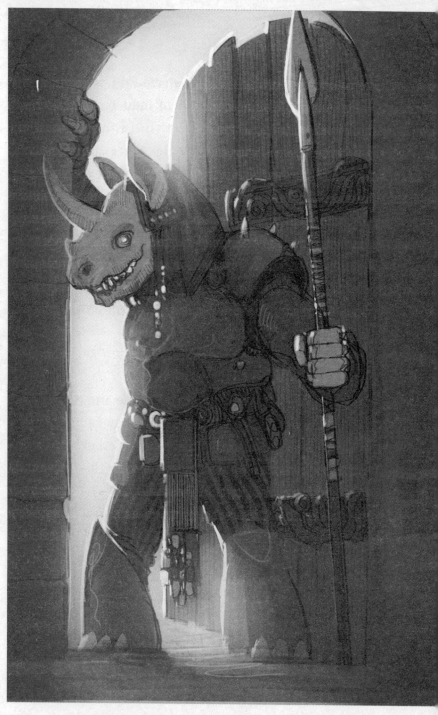

The door opens and a large, brutish creature steps out

118

The door opens and a large, brutish creature steps out. It has a sharp horn in the middle of its forehead and its skin appears to be armour-plated. It grunts to ask you what you want and demands the password before letting you in. Do you know the password? If so, turn to **273**. If not, you will have to bluff your way in (turn to **198**).

119

You turn to face the powerful sorcerer. But he has disappeared! You spin round to see him standing behind you with a sharp dagger poised to strike. You try to spring out of the way, but it is too late. The blade sinks into your back. . .

You have failed in your mission.

120

You taste the wine and nod. The vintage is indeed excellent with a refreshing, fruity taste. You try a little more and start to feel light-headed. You may add 2 *STAMINA* points and 3 *LUCK* points for finding such an excellent beverage. You thank the Elf and press onwards. Turn to **95**.

121

As you run at the door, it suddenly opens in front of you. Unable to stop yourself, you rush headlong forwards into the room, eventually tripping over and rolling to a stop. Lose 1 *STAMINA* point for grazing your knee on the rocky floor. Turn to **257**.

122

You try a simple ruse to fool her, but she does not fall for it. She will stop you getting any further unless you use your magic. Turn to **47**.

123

You concentrate and images from the Calacorm flash through your mind. You see a plate full of dead shakes, then a similar-looking creature with greyish skin – possibly the female of its species – then you feel a great sense of pleasure as you see an unfortunate creature bound to the wall having its toes tickled with a burning torch. Then you see the plate of snakes again. Evidently this creature thinks about little but the simple pleasures of its miserable life and you will not learn much about how to escape. You had better try a Fool's Gold Spell (turn to **211**) or an Illusion Spell (turn to **35**). If you have neither, turn to **283**.

124

As the drape falls, daylight streams in through the window. You realize that you have lost all track of time since entering the Citadel. The sun is a welcome relief after your many hours of darkness. A thump makes you turn back towards your adversary. He is lying in a heap on the ground. You take a step forwards and he lets out a blood-curdling scream! 'The curtain!... You fool!...' he gasps in a voice that is obviously weak and dying. Evidently the daylight you have let in is sapping his strength rapidly, and he is trying desperately to crawl into the shadows. But he is too weak to move far and he slumps to the ground, face downwards. Turn to **400**.

125

As you break into a run, three arrows fly out towards you from nowhere. *Test your Luck.* If you are Lucky, they all miss and you arrive at the monument, ducking behind the stone. If you are Unlucky, one of the arrows sinks into your shoulder causing you 5 *STAMINA* points of damage before you reach the shelter of the monument. Turn to **209**.

126

You pause to consider, in a state of panic. Ahead, the passageway forks to the left and to the right. As you are trying to decide which direction to take, three creatures emerge from the left-hand passage. Calling the noises you heard 'footsteps' was not entirely accurate, as you will see. Turn to **316**.

127

She lifts her head and calls into the air. You stop in your tracks as you see the washing on the line rustle and kick about in the air. Freeing themselves from the line, several pieces of clothing wisp through the air towards you and, as they get close, you can make out ghostly bodies with long-dead faces inside the clothes. 'Protect me, my sons and daughters!' she cries – and suddenly the clothes are all around you. Some whip their sleeves at you, stinging you painfully. One pair of arms wraps itself around your neck, making it difficult to breathe and tightening its grip. You are flailing about with your sword, but doing little damage to the GHOSTS. The stranglehold is tightening and you will have to use your magic to get free, unless you have something in your backpack to offer the woman. Will you:

Offer her some Small Berries?   Turn to **53**
Offer her a Silver Mirror?   Turn to **387**
Use a Fire Spell?   Turn to **240**

If you have none of these turn to **194**.

128

As the Spell takes its effect, you begin to get various thoughts as they flash through the creature's mind. Apart from a feeling of fear that its captain might find out it was asleep at its post and let an intruder in, it holds some strange reverence for a carved Hairbrush which is apparently in the room somewhere. But this is all you receive and you must now defend yourself from its attack with something. Will you use:

Your sword?	Turn to **336**
A Fool's Gold Spell?	Turn to **36**
A Creature Copy Spell?	Turn to **262**
A Weakness Spell?	Turn to **152**

129

You struggle with the box for some time, trying to open it. It will not open. You take out your sword and strike the box, but you succeed only in blunting your sword – from now on you must deduct 1 point from your *SKILL* score. You do not manage to open the box. Will you:

Try to open the first box?	Turn to **260**
Try to open the third box?	Turn to **370**
Leave the boxes and press onwards?	Turn to **237**

130

The spell has no effect. Cross it off your list and draw your sword. Turn to **333**.

131

You quickly unsheathe the sword, pointing it towards the Leprechaun. He throws a glance at the blade and to your horror it droops limply from the hilt, hanging downwards like a leather belt. It seems that you won't get too far acting aggressively. Perhaps you had better ask him the way onwards. Turn to **348**.

132

You enter a room which is evidently a library of some sort. Books stretch from ceiling to floor on each wall and several tables and chairs are lined down the centre of the room. At the far end sits a dark-skinned man who looks up at you from a book over narrow eyeglasses. Behind him is a door. 'Yes, what is it?' he snaps. 'Which book are you looking for?' You scan the various shelves, which are labelled. Will you ask him for:

Biographies of Balthus Dire?	Turn to **18**
Secrets of the Black Tower?	Turn to **238**
Creatures of the Kingdom of Craggen Rock?	Turn to **375**

133

You cast your Spell. With your new-found strength you leap easily to the centre of the room over the trench and break open the lock on the chest. You curse as you find nothing inside but a good weight of lead shot. Quickly, you leap back across the trench towards the other door, as the spell is wearing off. *Test your Luck.* If you are Lucky, turn to **206**. If you are Unlucky, turn to **82**.

134

They are taken aback by your audacity. Rather than waiting for them to talk, you act aggressively and demand to know how to get into the Citadel. They point to the main entrance, obviously a little bewildered by your confident manner, and whisper amongst themselves. The Orc tells you that you will need the password, 'Scimitar', to get in. You ask about the vial of liquid within the box, whereupon they get agitated. Will you press them for more information about the vial (turn to **60**), leave them and head for the two men you saw earlier (turn to **269**), or press on towards the Black Tower (turn to **245**)?

135

Miks are masters of illusion, able to change themselves into any shape or form they wish. It is not certain what their true nature is, as few have seen them in their natural form, but they have been described by fairly reliable sources as a thin, Elf-like race. They are an aggressive lot, but their favoured weapon is a Needleknife (a thin stiletto-like dagger) with which they can only attack from close range. Although they can change themselves into any form – man, beast or object – they are unable to use metal in their disguises. They are also unable to cast their illusions over other objects. Turn to **326**.

136

They all protest strongly, but you explain that you have your orders and begin to snoop around the kitchen. Will you investigate:

The cupboards?	Turn to **17**
The broth in the kettle?	Turn to **167**
The roasting spit?	Turn to **389**

137

The man is old and has been hit about the head with a club of some sort. He asks for medicine but you have none. You could use a Stamina Spell to fix him up and he offers to help you if you will. If you will use your magic, turn to **383**. If not, you will have to leave him and continue along the wall (turn to **14**).

138

'What do I want with that?' she exclaims. Again her eyes turn deep red and the jets of fire shoot towards you. Will you cast a Shielding Spell (turn to **376**) or leave the room and head down the corridor for the middle room (turn to **64**)?

139

All three knives miss and stick deep into the door behind you. The Wheelies are almost on you and you must decide quickly whether to fight them (turn to **346**) or cast a Spell. You may cast either:

An Illusion Spell	Turn to **244**
A Fire Spell	Turn to **28**

140

You leave the room and head down a short corridor. Some metres down you find yourself at the foot of a staircase. This is a spiral staircase which leads right up into the Citadel Tower. You climb the stairs cautiously and eventually arrive on a small landing with two doorways in front of you. Will you take the left-hand door (turn to **25**) or the right-hand door (turn to **104**)?

141

The liquid tastes salty and you break into a cold sweat as it goes down. You begin to tremble and try to steady yourself on the altar. However, you trip forward, knocking the other two chalices onto the floor, spilling the other liquids. You slump to the floor yourself, feeling extremely ill and hazy. As if in a dream, you see a vision of a strange, muscular creature with two heads, a long tail, and scaly grey skin. In its hand it holds a large bunch of keys. A mouse runs across the table at which it is sitting and it shrieks loudly... The cry wakes you up with a start and you realize where you are. You pick yourself up and grope for the door handle – you must have some fresh air! You leave the chamber, rest for a few moments outside, and set off for the Citadel. Turn to **156**.

142

You try the handle and it turns. You can hear nothing coming from inside the room, so you open the door to look around. The room is small, with a golden candlestick on a table ... but suddenly, you hear a creaking sound coming from the floor! Too late, you realize that the stones beneath your feet are shifting to reveal a trap! You fall feet first into a pit. As you hit the bottom you roll sideways, down another passage, and continue rolling downwards. Try as you might, you cannot stop yourself rolling head-over-heels until eventually you come to a halt in a small chamber. But the shock has been too much for you. As the world goes black around you, you hear excited chatterings, then you pass out. Turn to **234**.

143

You concentrate and cast your Spell. A Hydra's torso appears, but that is all. The creature is so large that a single Spell will not create a duplicate. If you have another Creature Copy Spell, you may use it (turn to **360**), otherwise you may look in your backpack for something to use (turn to **226**). If you cannot, or will not use either of these, turn to **184**.

Poking your head round the door, you can see rows and rows of racks full of bottles

144

The door opens and you enter a narrow corridor. You follow it for some time until you finally come to another door: this time a wide, carved door with the inscription 'Wine Cellar' set into it. You try the handle and it opens. Poking your head round the door you can see rows and rows of racks full of bottles ... full of wine? The room is dimly lit by several candles. Your opening the door has caused a little bell to ring, and a figure is limping towards you up one of the aisles. Will you draw your sword and prepare to defend yourself (turn to **154**), or see what this fellow might have to say (turn to **56**)?

145

You draw your sword and leap across the table at him. He, meanwhile, is evidently straining to fight off your Weakness Spell ... or is he? He buries his head in his hands and turns away from you. Turn to **80**.

146

You may ask one favour of them. Will you:

Ask how you may defeat Balthus Dire?	Turn to **247**
Ask where the doors ahead lead to?	Turn to **201**
Ask how to avoid the Ganjees?	Turn to **102**
Tell them you are a little weary – is there anything they could do?	Turn to **66**

147

The Golem crashes to the ground and breaks into pieces. With relief, you walk over to the boxes to examine them. Will you try to open:

The first box?	Turn to **260**
The second box?	Turn to **129**
The third box?	Turn to **370**

148

The sorcerer snorts with contempt. 'Then you can blame your death on those same countryfolk who sent you on this task!' With these words, he pulls a sharp dagger from his belt and drives it into your chest. You have failed in your quest.

149

They are not interested in your company and bid you on your way. You may either carry on towards the Tower (turn to **245**), turn to the left to investigate the monument in the centre of the courtyard (turn to **209**), or sit down at the fire anyway (turn to **380**).

150

You duck quickly to avoid the Trident. It misses your neck but glances off your forehead. Lose 2 *STAMINA* points and turn to **374**.

151

The suits of armour are a variety of shapes and sizes and you shiver to think of the strange creatures they must have been made for; perhaps you may yet come across some of them. As you examine one particularly grand suit, its hand suddenly rises and whacks you across the face! You stagger back, spitting blood. Lose 2 *STAMINA* points. But the armour makes no further move, and you decide it may be prudent to continue upstairs, either up the left-hand staircase (turn to **19**), or up the right-hand staircase (turn to **197**).

152

You cast your Spell and the creature stops in its tracks, not quite sure what has happened to it. With some effort it picks up its axe and comes towards you, but is evidently not such a strong adversary as before. You draw out your sword to finish the Gark off.

GARK   *SKILL* 5   *STAMINA* 5

If you defeat the creature, turn to **180**.

153

You are powerless against the Gorgon. You slump helplessly in the corner, while the sorcerer summons his guards, who appear several minutes later. They pick you up and march you out of the room. Their leader asks the sorcerer for instructions. 'Execute the peasant!' is his reply.

You have failed in your mission.

154

As you draw your sword, the figure stops and takes something from the pouch at his waist. As he limps closer you can see that this creature is a BLACK ELF; tall and thin, with arrowhead ears and one lame leg. In his hand he holds a small device of some sort. He sees you, manipulates the device, and suddenly it becomes a stiletto sword in his hand! Will you advance and fight (turn to **275**) or lower your sword and talk to him (turn to **56**)?

155

Your hand goes for your sword hilt. You draw out the blade. But you do not strike the sorcerer. Your own will compels you to offer him the weapon, which you do. He accepts. Turn to **65**.

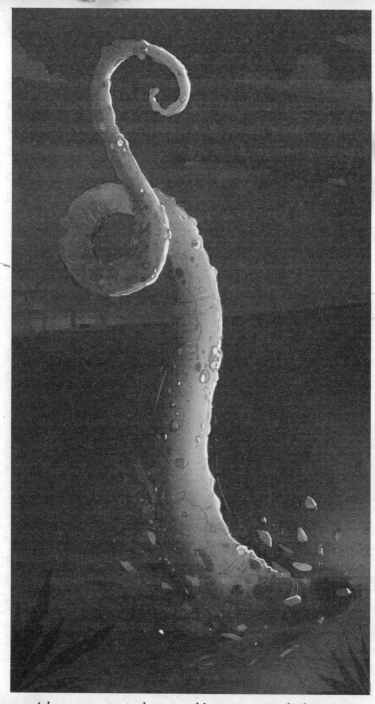

A long, grey tentacle covered in warty growths bursts out of the ground and wraps itself around your leg

156

As you stride across the open courtyard, you notice that you are walking alongside a small mound, almost like a buried pipeline running from the Black Tower to the temple. You bend over to investigate it; could it perhaps have been made by a mole of some kind? As you touch the mound, it caves in and, to your horror, a long, grey tentacle covered in warty growths bursts out of the ground and wraps itself around your leg! How will you fight this 'thing':

Draw your sword?	Turn to **71**
Cast a Levitation Spell?	Turn to **284**
Cast a Fire Spell?	Turn to **114**

157

The sorcerer cries out in anguish and turns away from you, holding his head. You rush forward and he wheels round to face you. You gasp! He is no longer the demi-sorcerer but has changed into a wicked-faced hag with wrinkled skin. His – or rather *her* – hair is now a squirming mass of hissing serpents! Will you press an attack (turn to **199**), or retreat quickly (turn to **232**)?

158

The beast whimpers as the spell takes effect. The immense weight is indeed a burden without its normal strength. It collapses in a heap, unable even to lift itself from the ground. You step over and run your sword through its chest. The unfortunate creature lies dead at your feet. Turn to **77**.

159

You cast your Weakness Spell. Hopefully, you wait for the creature's strength to fade. But as its teeth still maul you, you are dismayed to find that its attack is becoming more ferocious. You cannot feel your leg now. The pain is intense. You feel faint and lose consciousness as the jaws close on your throat. Turn to **323**.

160

The Dog-Head flies towards you and snatches the gadget from your hand. Examining it, the other two creatures gather round. They seem fascinated by it. While they are so preoccupied, you may creep through the room to the door in the far corner. Turn to **206**.

161

She is deeply insulted by your indifference. The Whirlwind rises once more and this time she knocks you off your feet. You try crawling forward, but she positions herself in front of you in whichever direction you turn. You will have to try to outwit her, but how will you start:

Make your anger obvious
to her?   Turn to **106**
Talk to her to try to pacify her?   Turn to **390**

162

You feel power surge through your body. The creatures see your rippling muscles harden in front of their eyes and stop dead in their tracks. Your hand grabs at your sword hilt and you whip out your blade. But to your despair, your new strength is difficult to control and your first slash with the sword sends the blade flying through the air to land several metres away! The creatures grin at each other and advance. You will now have to face them bare-handed, or you may use your new strength to bound away down the hillside.

If you wish to fight, the creatures' scores are (fight them in turn):

	SKILL	STAMINA
APE-DOG	7	4
DOG-APE	6	6

Treat your scores as normal. You may indeed have super-strength, but you are unarmed. If you win, you may retrieve your sword. Your strength returns to normal. Turn to **32**.

If you wish to run away, do so, and start again tomorrow night. Whichever you choose, remember to cross off the Strength Spell you have just used.

163

You take a sip and gag. This wine is awful! The Elf is looking on expectantly and you must not insult him, so you take another sip, grimacing as the liquid goes down. You thank him very much but explain quickly that you must be getting back. You head for the far end of the room but your stomach will take the horrid taste no longer. You are violently ill on the way out. Lose 1 *SKILL* and 2 *STAMINA* points for your nausea and turn to **95**.

164

The door is solid metal and no amount of charging, even with a Strength Spell, will budge it. You fall to your knees. After having come so far, your mission has failed. Unable to go on, you will have to try again; this time looking for the combination on the way through. You may, if you have one, use a Levitation Spell to take you away out of the Citadel. You will have to try again, tomorrow night...

165

As you feel the strength surging through your body, you draw out your sword and dig into the earthy walls. By making a foothole, then stepping on to it as you dig the next, you make your way up the shaft quite quickly with your boost of power. Halfway up, however, your strength begins to ebb and you realize you are returning to normal. If you allow this to happen, you will fall backwards into the pit once more. You may either cast another Strength Spell to give you the energy to complete your staircase (turn to **398**), or you may shout for help (turn to **202**).

166

As you bite into the meat, you hear a faint squeal of pain coming from somewhere distant. The meat is tough and salty, but does not taste too bad, so you take another bite. Again you hear a cry and this time the joint of meat flies from your hand! As you pick it up it pulls at your grip. You realize that this meat is still alive, and is screaming as you eat it! You feel a stab of pain in your stomach, then another. The two mouthfuls you have eaten are trying to fight their way out of your body! You fall to the ground, clutching your belly.

The meat will have three 'attacks' on your stomach

before it is digested. Throw two dice three times. Each time the number thrown is higher than your *SKILL* score, deduct 2 *STAMINA* points. If *all three* throws exceed your *SKILL* score, then the damage it does will be fatal and this is the end of your adventure. If you survive, you may leave either by the door in the left-hand wall (turn to **13**), or the door opposite the one you came through (turn to **281**).

167

You bend over the broth and take a sniff. Phew! It is revolting! You ask them what on earth it is, and as you look up, you can see that one of them has been quietly waving her hands at the broth. You pull your head back, but too late. A large SNAPPERFISH rises from the broth and snaps its sharp teeth at your head. *Test your Luck*. If you are Lucky, turn to **224**. If you are Unlucky, turn to **331**.

168

You take out the Amulet and place it over your head. The Ganjees gasp! 'Begone stranger,' says a voice. 'We will not bother you. Take the door in the far corner.' With those words, a door in the corner of the room glows slightly. You walk over to it and open the door. Turn to **328**.

169

The room you are in is some sort of grand dining hall. A long table, large enough to seat some forty or fifty people, stands in the centre, edged with chairs. Various doors and passageways lead from the room, but you are particularly interested in two wide staircases which lead upwards to either end of a balcony overlooking the hall. Paintings and suits of armour decorate the walls. The room is empty. Will you:

Take the left-hand staircase upwards?	Turn to **19**
Take the right-hand staircase upwards?	Turn to **197**
Investigate the paintings?	Turn to **317**
Investigate the suits of armour?	Turn to **151**

170

As the strength surges into your body, you charge the door with all your might. Roll one die. If you roll a 1,2 or 3, the door does not break and you must lose 2 *STAMINA* points. If you roll a 4, 5 or 6, you break the door down (turn to **292**). Continue this until you succeed, or you may decide to try either the middle door (turn to **64**), or the far door (turn to **304**) instead.

171

For this game you will need at least 1 Gold Piece. If you haven't any Gold Pieces, you may use a Fool's Gold Spell and take your Fool's Gold to the Games Master, who will give you 10 Gold Pieces for it. (If you have no Gold Pieces or Fool's Gold Spells, you cannot play the game.) Choose any numbers you wish between 1 and 6 and stake any number of your Gold Pieces on each one. Write your selection(s) and stake(s) down. Then roll one die. If the number you roll is one of your choices, you win five times the stake you have placed on that number. You may continue as long as you like, or you may switch to playing Knifey-Knifey (turn to **365**), or Runestones (turn to **278**). If you are bored with playing games, turn to **31**. But you must play at least one game of Six Pick, if you have Gold Pieces or a Fool's Gold Spell, before you move on.

172

You advance and take a swing at the creature. With a clang, your sword bounces off its stone body. Realizing that you cannot harm it with your weapon, you may either cast a Spell (turn to **26**), or use something from your backpack (turn to **289**).

173

You concentrate hard, and a green, fuming gas jets out of your finger towards the creature. She realizes that her own spinning will suck the gas inside her Whirlwind and begins to back off. When she has retreated far enough, you make a dash for the Black Tower. Turn to **218**.

174

The passageway twists and turns, eventually ending in a flight of stairs going upwards. You climb the stairs and find yourself in a short passage ending at a dead end. As you examine the wall, you discover a short lever, which you pull. The rock face ahead opens slightly and closes behind you as you walk through. You are now standing in front of a door, which is locked. Will you try to break it down (turn to **268**) or will you cast a Strength Spell to smash it to bits (turn to **116**)?

175

The creature has never heard of a Pincus within the Citadel. The Dog-Ape holding the mace growls and steps forward. You may quickly choose another name (turn to **110**) or may prepare to fight them (turn to **288**).

176

As you get closer, she turns to look at you. Not in the least perturbed by your weapon, she says, 'Put down your weapon, young stranger. I am but an old woman. I'll do you no harm.' Will you do as she asks?

If you ignore her words and
continue advancing   Turn to **127**
If you put away your sword
and talk to her   Turn to **21**
If you stop and use
an E.S.P. Spell   Turn to **329**

177

You are in a narrow hallway. This continues for several metres and ends in a doorway. Halfway along the passage you can see an archway where some steps lead downwards. Will you go forwards to the door (turn to **5**), or creep down the steps (turn to **344**)?

178

You run around the kitchen, followed by the Devlin. You throw chairs, food, knives and bowls at it, but all have no effect. You sling a cup of liquid across the room and, to your surprise, the Devlin shrieks as it hits its flaming body! Then you get an idea. Nipping over to the kettle of broth, you dodge the creature until the two of you are running round the kettle, just out of each other's reach. You both stop, facing each other across the steaming brew. With a great heave, you tip the contents of the kettle out – all over the creature, which screams and disappears as its flames are extinguished. Now you may either check the cupboards (turn to **17**), or leave through the door at the far end of the kitchen (turn to **265**).

179

As you step out of the shadows towards the centre of the courtyard, a voice in the wind cries, 'Halt! Stand your ground!' You whirl about but can see no-one addressing you. You take another couple of steps. Again, the eerie voice orders you to stop, and this time an arrow zings through the air and lands close to your left foot. You jump back. Still you can see no-one. But now you are stuck. Will you:

Press on forwards, very cautiously?	Turn to **378**
Make a dash for the monument in the centre of the yard?	Turn to **125**
Cast a Shielding Spell around yourself and advance?	Turn to **341**

180

The great Gark lies dead on the ground. You wait for a minute to see whether the commotion will attract any guards, but all appears to be safe. You go through the creature's effects, but find little of value. Inside a pouch strung around its waist are 6 Gold Pieces and an ornate Hairbrush. You may take these with you if you wish. You decide to continue onwards. Turn to **99**.

Suddenly, a ghostly white luminous face flies towards you

181

You cast the Spell into the air. As you do so, the Flying Carpet sails past you and, to your consternation, a second, identical carpet appears and begins to fly around the room. Suddenly the air is awhirl. The Dog Head flies off the wall and bites your arm savagely. Lose 2 *STAMINA* points. The man, who has turned into a Snake, slithers up to you and lunging forwards, strikes at your leg. *Test your Luck*. If you are Lucky, the Snake's fangs merely graze you. Lose another 2 *STAMINA* points. If you are Unlucky, its fangs sink deep into your calf and your leg begins to throb with pain. In a blinding flash you realize that the bite is deadly and you sink to the ground clutching your wound and writhing in agony. As the poison takes effect, your head swims and consciousness fades. You have failed in your mission. If you have survived, though fortunate, you are not unscarred. Your body is wracked with pain and you must either offer your opponents a gift from your backpack (turn to **54**), or leave the room quickly by the other door (turn to **25**).

182

You feel yourself sucked into the room. As if by magic, your torch flickers and dies. The room is pitch black. From nowhere, yet everywhere, comes a mocking laugh which fills the room. 'Foolish adventurer,' says another voice, which changes its tone from high to low as it speaks, 'Welcome to the home of the GANJEES! Unfortunately, it will be the last room you will ever see... Ah, but of course, you cannot see, can you? But *we* can see *you*, can't we brothers?' And laughing voices come from all around you. Suddenly a ghostly white luminous face flies towards you. You recoil in horror, throwing yourself on the ground, and begin to feel very frightened. Lose 1 *SKILL*, 2 *STAMINA* and 1 *LUCK* point for your fear. What can you do here:

Create a Fire Spell?   Turn to **85**
Try an Illusion Spell?   Turn to **395**
Feel in your backpack for
an artefact?   Turn to **322**
Draw your sword?   Turn to **248**

He thanks you profusely. You have made a friend here. Turn to **270**.

184

While you are deliberating your next move, the Hydra advances. Two of its heads dart out and bite you; one on your arm and the other on your neck. Its sharp teeth pierce your skin and bite deep. All is lost. You have failed in your mission.

185

The door opens into a narrow corridor which bends round sharply to the left, continues for several metres, then ends finally at a door. You grasp the handle. Turn to **13**.

186

The tall man agrees and persuades the shorter man that this is a fair price. The short man mumbles and curses, offering 6, then 7, Gold Pieces but the price has been fixed at 8. You may, if you wish, offer the tall man 8 Gold Pieces yourself, although you will have to conjure up some Fool's Gold to give to him. If you want to do this, use up a Fool's Gold Spell and turn to **15**. If not, the short man eventually agrees to the price, buys the dagger and leaves. You may remain to talk to the tall man (turn to **83**), or may continue on your way (turn to **245**).

187

You concentrate on the sorcerer's mind. Images and words flash through your head. A couple of seconds later, there is nothing. You look up at Balthus Dire, who is glaring at you. 'Do not try to probe the mind of Balthus Dire!' he commands. You concentrate again, but still receive nothing as he is now blocking your Spell. You reflect for a second on the images you did receive: a chart under the battle plan table ... a sense of horror at a high-pitched screech ... a blinding light ... a ring on his finger ... a razor-edged sword ... and you.

He is now mumbling under his breath, watching you with one eye. He raises one hand in the air and concentrates his gaze on it. Then he looks at you. He waves his hand in the air, backwards and forwards and side to side, faster and faster. With a crash he brings his hand down on the table. You fall to the floor – not in surprise, but because the ground beneath you is shaking violently. The whole room seems to be tossing like a ship in a tempest. Although he has a firm footing and is now walking towards you, you cannot rise to your feet at all. Your only chance is a Spell, if you have any left. If so, will you use:

A Levitation Spell?   Turn to **279**

An Illusion Spell? Turn to **314**

But if you have neither of these, turn to **115**.

188

A sudden intense flash of light bursts out in front of you. You shield your eyes and then rub them – but you cannot see! Panic hits you as you hear a low growling noise. Padded footsteps come closer and you cry out in pain as this unseen creature roars and embeds its sharp teeth in your leg. Will you:

Cast a Strength Spell? Turn to **301**

Cast a Weakness Spell? Turn to **159**

Draw your sword and slash out
at the creature? Turn to **51**

189

You may use any of the following Spells:

Illusion Spell Turn to **319**

Shielding Spell Turn to **130**

Weakness Spell Turn to **43**

If you have none of these, you will have to use your sword. Turn to **333**.

190

A perfect copy of the Golem forms in front of you. You command it to attack the real Golem, which is now almost upon you. Resolve the battle of the Golems:

GOLEM   *SKILL 8*   *STAMINA 10*

If your creation beats the original, turn to **147**. If it does not, you will have to finish off the fight yourself. If you win, you may also turn to **147**.

191

You gasp as the Spell materializes itself in front of you. A perfect replica of yourself, armed as you are, now stands in front of you. At the sorcerer's command, your twin advances and you must fight it. It has the same *SKILL, STAMINA* and *LUCK* scores as you have. The only advantage you may have is by using your *LUCK* to do extra damage or minimize wounds – your twin will not use its *LUCK* here. If you win, turn to **119**.

192

You cast the Spell just in time. The missile hits your magical shield and splatters against it, dribbling on to the floor. You test the resulting mush to see what it was. You were nearly hit by a tomato! In the centre of the room, the sleeping figure is stirring. Turn to **29**.

193

Choose a Spell:

Fool's Gold	Turn to **211**
E.S.P.	Turn to **123**
Illusion	Turn to **35**

If you have none of these, turn to **283**.

194

The stranglehold around your neck tightens and your last living memory is one of fear – of these non-human creatures with their long-dead faces, gloating over your death.

You have failed in your mission.

195

Balthus' eyes follow you as you duck but you are obscured by the battle plan table. The miniature fireball dips in the air but shoots over your head. You may quickly use another Spell to attack. Turn to **377**.

196

The room is indeed a food store. At first, the strange smells – a mixture of sweet, spicy and stale food – take you by surprise. Various meats hang on hooks along one wall. In one corner is a barrel, full of exotic fruits. A cheese rack holds a dozen or so varieties of cheese and your nose turns up in disgust at the strong smell of the, shall we say, 'over-ripe' ones. Six loaves of black bread stand on a table, next to a bread knife and cutting board. Two other doors lead from the room. If you are hungry, you may try some of the food (turn to **45**), otherwise you may leave either through the door in the left-hand wall (turn to **13**), or the door in the right-hand wall (turn to **281**).

197

The stairs are well-worn and creak under your weight. Cautiously you climb up to the balcony. Turn to **363**.

198

You think quickly. You reach into your bag and pull out a handful of weeds. Showing them to the creature, you explain that you are a herbalist and have come to treat the Lord's librarian, who is critically ill. The messenger never told you of any passwords. Will he believe you? *Test your Luck*. If you are Lucky, he believes you and lets you in (turn to **177**). If you are Unlucky, he doesn't care who you are, you may not enter without the password, and he advances towards you with his pike (turn to **290**).

199

The sorcerer has transformed himself into a GORGON, an extremely dangerous creature with the power to turn to stone any who catch her gaze. As you lunge forward you stare directly into her face and her Spell is cast. You can feel your joints stiffening. You fall to the floor. Your consciousness fades as you turn into a stone statue, dead at the feet of Balthus Dire. . .

You have failed in your mission.

200

At your first movement, the creature seems to break from its trance and steps towards you. Seeing this you may either run for the door at the far end of the room (turn to **237**), or make for the boxes and risk taking on this silent giant (turn to **98**).

201

They point towards the two doors. The one on the left, they say, takes you into the kitchen, where the cooks will be preparing the supper. The door on the right leads into the Great Hall, where all the banquets are held. Turn to **270**.

202

After several minutes of shouting, you hear voices in a strange tongue coming closer. To your relief you see four heads peering into the pit, silhouetted against the sky. You yell at them to get some rope. They chatter and disappear. Eventually you hear their scurrying footsteps returning. They stand once more at the top of the pit and throw down to you, not a rescue rope, but the contents of a cauldron of boiling oil! You will have to watch your footing on your next adventure, for this one is over.

And remember – strangers are not welcome at the Citadel of Chaos...

203

As you race for the doors, you stumble, allowing the creature to gain ground. It grabs your arm with one hand and throws you across the room; you land with a crash against the wall under the mirror. You will now either have to draw your sword (turn to **16**), or prepare to use a Spell (turn to **11**).

204

You hold your nose and step forward into the slimy water. A couple of steps in, you feel a pulling on your leg. Lifting it out of the water you find that some sort of vine has coiled itself around your leg. You leap back to the bank and the vine remains fixed. From out of the water, one end of the vine rises, moves around in the air as if looking at you, and then falls back with a splash. You realize that this is not a vine, but a long SEWER SNAKE, which is now pulling itself towards you. Turn to **73**.

205

The tall man is outraged by your price, but the other agrees. The argument becomes more intense and the taller man draws his sword. The shorter man does likewise and, as you are threatened, so do you. It is you and the shorter man against the tall man. You must resolve this battle. Before starting each *Attack Round,* roll one die. If the number is odd, the tall man will attack the shorter man first and you personally may ignore that *Attack Round* (although you must still roll for the short man). If the number is even, the tall man goes for you (and the shorter man can ignore that *Attack Round*). If the shorter man dies during the battle, the taller man will finish off the battle with you.

	SKILL	STAMINA
TALL MAN	8	8
SHORT MAN	7	6

When the battle has been resolved, turn to **309** if the shorter man is still alive. If he has been killed, turn to **368**.

206

You leave through the door and find yourself at the foot of another spiral staircase leading up into the Black Tower. Climbing the stairs, you eventually come to a landing where a single door is the only way onwards. You try the door. It opens slowly. Turn to **182**.

207

You open the door and peer through into the darkness beyond. You walk a couple of paces forward, allowing your eyes to accustom themselves to the blackness. You close the door behind you, bidding the Leprechaun farewell. Turn to **188**.

208

The Spider-Man's weapon is its bite, which is highly poisonous. As it bites you, you feel the poison spreading through your system, numbing your nerves. As you stumble and fall to the ground, it attacks you again and again. Your last memory is its ugly little face biting into your neck.

You have failed in your mission.

*Hovering above the table – fast asleep – is a very
small man dressed in a green shirt and pantaloons*

209

You cast your eyes over the strange structure. It appears not to be a fountain, but a temple of some sort. To one side there is a door, which you may investigate, or you may press onwards towards the Citadel itself. If you wish to press onwards, turn to **156**. If you wish to investigate, turn to **362**.

210

You now stand in a large, round room. It is lit by a single torch, fixed into one wall. There is no furniture in the room, save for a rough wooden table and chair in the centre. Hovering above the table – fast asleep – is a very small man dressed in a green shirt and pantaloons. He cannot be more than a metre tall and you cannot believe that he is still asleep after your noisy entrance! You hear a creak and turn to your right in time to see a small catapult fire a missile of some sort straight at you. It is going to hit you unless you use a Shielding Spell! If you use this Spell, turn to **192**. If you cannot (or will not), turn to **359**.

211

You offer him the pebbles you have turned into gold. 'Everything I want is down here,' he says. 'I am fed, I have a job to do and, if I get bored I am allowed to torture the prisoners for amusement. What do *I* want with gold?' You had better try another Spell. Will you go for an E.S.P. Spell (turn to **123**), or an Illusion Spell (turn to **35**)? If you have neither of these, turn to **283**.

212

Taking the left fork, you follow a path which eventually joins another passageway leading on northwards. You follow this new path for some distance until it eventually widens out. Turn to **90**.

213

You draw your sword just in time, as the Dwarf is almost upon you. Fight each in turn:

	SKILL	*STAMINA*
DWARF	5	6
GOBLIN	6	4
ORC	5	7

If you win, turn to **235**. You may *Escape* during the battle by making off for the monument in the centre of the courtyard (turn to **209**).

214

You take the stopper off the Vial and spray the creature with the green liquid. It growls and screams in the air, clutching itself around the neck. The liquid appears to be burning into the Gargoyle and fumes rise into the air. Moments later, the creature lies dead on the ground. Turn to **62**.

215

You will have to make up some story for these ugly women. Will you tell them that the Captain of the Guard has ordered an inspection of their kitchen after a couple of cases of food poisoning (turn to **136**), or will you tell them you have taken a wrong turn and you are looking for the way onwards (turn to **41**)?

216

What will your approach be? You may either tell the creature that you are a guest (turn to **294**), or you may try to bribe the Gark by offering it 3 Gold Pieces – *real* Gold Pieces – (turn to **391**), or by using a Fool's Gold Spell to create some gold to offer it (turn to **36**).

217

You turn the handle as carefully as possible so as to surprise whatever awaits you. Slowly, the door opens and you enter the room, which is dark and lit by a single flickering candle. Your blood drains as you see a three-pronged TRIDENT heading directly for your throat! In a flash you must decide what to do. Will you:

Immediately cast a Shielding Spell?	Turn to **293**
Try quickly to side-step the weapon?	Turn to **57**

218

In front of you is a large wooden door, firmly locked. You may either knock three times for the guard (turn to **118**), or you may use a Strength Spell to try to open it (turn to **94**).

219

You duck and cover your head. A bottle hits you, then another, then another – but you don't feel a thing! How could this be? Then you realize what is happening. The wine must have contained some hallucinatory potion that is making you imagine the bottle attack. In an instant, the noise ceases. You look up to see that, as you suspected, all the bottles are in place on their racks. With great relief, you press onwards and leave the Wine Cellar. Turn to **95**.

220

The knives hit your magic shield and drop to the ground. The Wheelies likewise bump into the shield and bounce off, somewhat mystified. They chatter to each other, holding you at bay while your Spell wears off. They seem to reach some sort of agreement and one rolls off back up the corridor, presumably to fetch help. The other two reach for their belts and pull out small blowpipes. Putting some kind of pellets in their mouths first, they prepare to aim. You will have to leap on them first with your sword. Resolve this battle (fight each in turn):

	SKILL	*STAMINA*
First WHEELIE	7	6
Second WHEELIE	6	5

If you win, you may take either the left-hand passage (turn to **243**), or the right-hand passage (turn to **2**).

221

As you move forwards, she makes a peculiar gesture with her hands and lowers her head, mumbling quietly. Turn to **127**.

*As you get closer, you can make out the shape
of a man on the ground, obviously in pain*

222

As you creep around the wall, you hear a low moaning noise a few metres ahead. As you get closer, you can make out the shape of a man on the ground, obviously in pain. He calls out for help. Will you approach him to see what you can do (turn to **137**) or ignore him and continue along the wall (turn to **14**)?

223

She grimaces as she looks at the ugly little thing, pulling the bedclothes up around her neck. Turn to **138**.

224

You quickly whip your head back and narrowly avoid the Snapperfish's jaws. But you crack your head on the handle on which the kettle is hanging. Lose 2 *STAMINA* points. You reel from the blow and, as you try to collect your senses, the three old women shove you off towards the door at the far end of the kitchen. 'Good riddance, scab!' they shout as they shove you through the door. Turn to **265**.

225

He agrees entirely. This artefact is extremely valuable. The shorter man explains that he just doesn't have that kind of money, and wanders off into the darkness. The tall man offers the dagger to you at the bargain price of 9 Gold Pieces. You may use a Fool's Gold Spell to conjure up enough gold to buy the knife (deduct this spell and turn to **15**) or you may apologize and press onwards (turn to **245**).

226

You may pull from your backpack any one of the following, if you have collected them:

A Silver Mirror	Turn to **312**
A Golden Fleece	Turn to **37**
A Pocket Myriad	Turn to **384**

If you have none of these, turn to **184**.

227

They begin to get very angry at your manner. Tempers rise and they start to shout. Suddenly you are overwhelmed by them. You struggle, but one of them cracks you on the head with a sword hilt. Your head swims and the room goes black as you lose consciousness. Turn to **234**.

228

The locked door is very strong and made of solid oak. It is unlikely you will break it down, but you may try. Otherwise you could use a Strength Spell to smash it. The lock is copper and you could try using a Copper Key if you have one. Which will you choose:

Try to smash it down?	Turn to **88**
Cast a Strength Spell?	Turn to **170**
Use a Copper Key?	Turn to **296**

229

You slam the door shut behind you. You follow a short, narrow passage, which winds round and brings you to the foot of another staircase, reaching right up into the apex of the Citadel. A sign on the wall reads 'HALT. None may pass but by order of Balthus Dire.' You realize you are nearing your goal. Cautiously you climb the stairs to the next landing, right up in the belfry of the Citadel. In front of you is a solid metal door. You try the handle but the door is locked. You lift a small flap and can see small tumblers underneath. This is a combination lock which can only be opened by those who know the combination. Do you know the combination? If so, turn to the section of the book with that same number. If not, you may either try to break the door down (turn to **50**), or use a Strength Spell (turn to **164**).

230

'Come to make some money, eh?' says the Ape-Dog. 'Well you can share some of your profits with us!' As you have nothing to offer them, you can pull a rock out of your pouch and cast a Fool's Gold Spell on it, offering them a gold nugget (turn to **96**), or you can prepare yourself for battle (turn to **288**). Deduct the Fool's Gold Spell from your Spells if you use it.

231

You barge the door with your shoulder. *Test your Luck*. If you are Lucky, the door breaks open (turn to **196**). If you are Unlucky, you bruise your shoulder – lose 1 *STAMINA* point – and you must *Test your Luck* again, repeating this procedure until you are Lucky.

Lose 1 *STAMINA* point for each unsuccessful attempt. When you do eventually break the door open, turn to **196**. Otherwise, if your shoulder is getting a little too painful, you may return to the first fork you came to and take the other passage at any time (turn to **243**).

232

You back off in horror from the hideous creature standing before you. From the legends you have been told in your youth you realize that you are facing a GORGON, whose gaze has the power to turn you to stone! *Test your Luck.* If you are Lucky, turn to **111**. If you are Unlucky, turn to **72**.

233

You avoid the full impact of the Trident, but one of its prongs embeds itself in your shoulder. Luckily it is not your sword arm. You grab the shaft and wrench it from your shoulder, crying out in pain as you do so. Lose 5 *STAMINA* points for your injury and turn to **374**.

*You can see a lizard-like creature shuffling
down the corridor, carrying a mug and bowl*

234

You wake up in a dirty room with rough walls cut into the rock. Iron bars in the window and the door confirm your suspicion that you are in a prison cell of some sort. There is not much you can do but sit on the straw mattress in one corner until someone appears. An hour or so later, you hear a shuffling noise outside. Looking through the bars in the door you can see a lizard-like creature shuffling down the corridor, carrying a mug and bowl. The beast has two heads which talk to each other as he walks. Its skin is grey and scaly and a long tail follows it up the passage. It stops at your door and pushes the bowl and mug through a small opening into your cell, then shambles off to sit at a table across the hall. You have been given bread and broth. Will you eat and drink, or will you call out to this creature, a CALACORM? To take your food, turn to **397**. If you wish to shout to the Calacorm, turn to **69**.

235

Afraid that the commotion may have attracted attention, you peer out into the darkness. Nothing seems to be happening. Going through the pockets of the creatures you find 8 Gold Pieces, a copper-coloured key, and a jar of a dark, creamy ointment. You may take any two of these with you. Turning to the vial of liquid, you can make out an inscription on the lid, written in runes. Your heart leaps as you realize that this is a Potion of Magik and is very rare. Within the vial is enough liquid for two doses, and each has the effect of raising your *MAGIC* score by 1 point, allowing you the energy to use one extra spell. You may take this Potion with you to use after using any Spell. When you drink the Potion, you need not cross that Spell off your list. Remember this Potion will only work twice. Now you may carry on, either towards the Citadel (turn to **245**), or over to the two men talking by torchlight (turn to **269**).

236

They take your Berries enthusiastically, popping them into their mouths and chewing them. Seconds later, they fall asleep, one by one. When all three are asleep, you walk over to investigate the box. The lid opens revealing several more dolls inside, just like the ones on the floor, and various other wooden toys. There seems to be nothing of real value there and so you leave the room by the far door. Turn to **140**.

237

You open the door and step forwards into a passageway, which runs eastwards for several metres and then ends at the foot of a staircase. You climb the stairs and eventually find yourself in a narrow passageway. A short distance ahead, you can see an opening into a large, well-lit room. You press on forwards. Turn to **169**.

He indicates a section on the shelves and you take a book to one of the tables to read through it. The book is most enlightening, tracing the history of the Citadel. The Black Tower was built by Balthus Dire's grandfather. As it became a sanctuary for the forces of evil, law and order gradually made way for chaos as the monstrous creatures battled their way up the power hierarchy. Dire's grandfather eventually found it necessary to protect himself from his minions by setting up various protective traps between the creatures and his own dwellings, most notable of these being the Doompit Trap and a magical Combination Lock on the door to his own room. The combination of the lock is 217. You read further about the various secret passageways that permeate the Citadel. You may then choose either to ask the man for the section on Balthus Dire (turn to **18**), or the section on Creatures of Craggen Rock (turn to **375**), or you may leave the room through the door at the far end (turn to **31**).

239

An idea strikes you. You tie the rope into a loop, with a slip-knot at the end. Whirling the rope around your head, you try to snare the chest. After several throws, your loop goes over the chest and the slip-knot tightens around it. You pull, and the chest shifts. You pull once, and it falls over the edge and down into the trench – but to your dismay, the weight of the box is enormous and it pulls you right over with it! If you have a Levitation Spell, use it and turn to **379**. Otherwise turn to **82**.

240

You hold up a flaming hand, running it down the back of the gown with its arms around your neck. The garment bursts into flames and a silent scream comes from the dead mouth within it. The other Ghosts back off. You set fire to a couple more as they retreat. Unluckily they are too close and you lose 2 *STAMINA* points for your burns. Walking carefully forward you hold the rest of the Ghosts at bay until you are safely past the woman. Turn to **6**.

241

You hit the creature a damaging blow. But to your dismay, your sword tangles itself within the beast's long hair. You try to pull, but it slashes at the sword and knocks it out of your hand across the room. You are now defenceless. You may either continue the fight with your bare hands, or cast a Strength Spell. If you fight at normal strength without a weapon, deduct 3 points from your *SKILL* score for the rest of the fight. If you use a Strength Spell, you may continue at normal *SKILL*. If you win, you may retrieve your sword and turn to **77**.

242

The bottles and caskets contain hundreds of different types of wine. Some are exceedingly old and valuable. In one corner of the room there is a table laid out for sampling, with two bottles and glasses.

Will you try a sample of the Red Wine (turn to **24**), or the White Wine (turn to **105**) or will you try neither and press onwards (turn to **95**)? If you decide to leave, you may take a bottle of wine off one of the racks with you for your journey.

243

The passage runs along for several metres and then ends at a door. You listen at the door and can hear a deep heavy breathing coming from inside, as if some large creature were asleep in there. Cautiously you try the handle and the door opens. Just inside, although the room is dark, you can see that a very large Goblin-like creature is asleep on the floor. You may either risk tiptoeing into the room (turn to **352**), or you may return to the fork and try the right-hand passage (turn to **2**).

244

As you concentrate on your Spell, the Wheelies stop. Evidently they are a little apprehensive about what you are planning. Suddenly, in front of their hairy eyes, you disappear! Again they chatter excitedly. Where have you gone to? Under your Invisibility Illusion, you may continue, choosing either the right-hand passageway (turn to **2**), or the left-hand passageway (turn to **243**) leaving the Wheelies to search around for you in vain.

You see a ghostly female face inside what appears to be a whirlwind

245

You set off towards the Citadel. Although the night air is calm, you hear a faint whistling, which rapidly gets louder and louder, until a strong gust of wind suddenly hits you with such a force that you can barely move against it. You shield your eyes until the blast retreats slightly and, as you open them, you see a ghostly female face inside what appears to be a living Whirlwind. She mouths words at you which you cannot make out, but some seconds after she has finished talking, the message reaches you. She seems to find your appearance offensive and is challenging you with words of abuse. You grab at your sword, but she laughs. Will you ignore her and continue (turn to **161**), talk to her (turn to **390**), or use your magic to see her off (turn to **47**)?

246

You disappear. You can, however, still watch the Calacorm from your cell. To your consternation, the beast has not noticed that you have gone! You wait patiently, but to no avail, and now you start to worry that the Spell will soon be wearing off. You kick the dust at your feet. The creature looks up and rushes over to your cell door. You are nowhere to be seen! It opens your door and enters the cell, but as it does so, your Spell begins to wear off. 'Try to trick me, eh?' says the Calacorm as it grabs you. You will now have to fight the creature:

CALACORM   *SKILL 9*   *STAMINA 8*

You may cast a Weakness Spell on it, which will reduce its *SKILL* to 5. If you defeat the creature, you may leave the jail along a passageway which runs northwards (turn to **174**).

247

They are shocked by your request. You curse as you realize you should not have let them know about your real mission. They all chatter excitedly for some time, then turn towards you. Together, they all blow hard. To your amazement, their breath is like a gale-force wind and you are hurled backwards against the wall. Your head cracks on the rough rocky wall and you lose consciousness. Turn to **234**.

248

A silence spreads over the room. Suddenly, a bloodcurdling scream comes from one corner and a hideous face appears in the air, shooting towards you, screaming as it comes. Your hair stands on end and your legs turn to jelly. Somehow, you manage to reach the door, fling it open and race through. However, you have forgotten that you are high in a tower and the balcony has no railing... You tumble over the ledge and fall straight down. If you have a Levitation Spell, turn to **103**. Otherwise you land in a crumpled heap at the base of the tower and your broken body breathes its last breath...

249

The passageway ends ahead of you at a wooden door. A sign reading 'PANTRY' is fixed to it. You listen but hear nothing. The door is locked. If you have a Copper Key you may try using it here (turn to **392**), otherwise you may either try to charge the door down (turn to **231**), or return to the fork and take the other passage (turn to **55**).

250

You concentrate and, before your eyes, a hurricane begins to swell up and ravage the room. Chairs, books and all sorts of things fly up into the air and are swirled around the room, leaving you untouched by the Illusion. You take a step forward but stop suddenly when you hear a loud laughing sound. You look into the room to see that the Flying Carpet and the Dog Head have changed into stone statues. One of them taunts you. 'We, my dear adventurer, are MIKS. We are *masters* of illusion. Your crude tricks cannot fool us!' The man, who has now turned into a Snake, has meanwhile slithered across the carpet, wrapped himself around your leg and is sinking his fangs into your rump. The pain is unbearable and you sink to the ground, realizing that the bite was poisonous. Beware of Miks in your next adventure. This one has ended here...

251

You walk forward into a spacious open courtyard surrounded by large walls. Various lights are burning and groups of figures are shuffling around in the darkness. In the centre of the courtyard is a large monument of some kind – perhaps a fountain. Looking across the yard you can see what appears to be the main entrance to the tower. Will you:

Creep around the wall towards the tower?	Turn to **222**
Stride boldly across the court yard?	Turn to **179**
Tiptoe through the shadows towards one of the groups?	Turn to **321**

252

You have snared either 5 or 6 of its heads! It struggles to free itself from the noose. With a snatch, the Myriad is wrenched from your hand. But nevertheless, the creature has been diverted enough to let you jump for the door on the far side of the room. Turn to **229**.

253

The cheese is indeed over-ripe, but as you eat it, you feel strangely refreshed. The taste, once inside your mouth, is most enjoyable and you take several mouthfuls. You may add 1 *SKILL* point, 3 *STAMINA* points and 1 *LUCK* point for this meal and then you can leave. If you will try the door in the left-hand wall, turn to **13**. If you wish to try the door opposite the one you came in through, turn to **281**.

254

You roll down the stairs, across the room and finally crash into the wall on the far side of the hall. You twist your elbow badly. Lose 1 *SKILL* and *2 STAMINA* points for your injuries and then take the other staircase up. Turn to **197**.

255

The creature looks at you. Its eyes narrow. In its hand is a long pike, which it quickly points towards you. 'That is not the password!' it bellows and steps out to do battle. *Test your Luck*. If you are Lucky, you think of a bluff quickly (turn to **198**). If you are Unlucky, you stammer and the creature advances to fight (turn to **290**).

256

The sorcerer smiles. 'Then you shall join me!' he laughs. 'But first I must secure your genuine loyalty.' His hand settles on your forehead. He closes his eyes and concentrates. You feel your will draining. Your fighting spirit is leaving you. After several moments he releases his grip. You stand free in front of him. Will you bow down and salute him as your master (turn to **65**), or grab your sword and run him through (turn to **155**)?

Your torch lights up a large creature, seemingly made of rock itself, standing by the door

257

You look round the room. It is lit only by your torch. Although a fairly large room, it has little furniture in it, although a large boulder, sliced flat, resembles a table and a smaller rock forms a sort of stool behind it. In one corner, a pile of rocks are held together with mud. You cannot imagine their purpose, although they support three wooden chests. Then you jump with fright as your torch lights up a large creature, seemingly made of rock itself, standing by a door. It is roughly human-shaped, although somewhat larger. Its eyes are staring straight at you, but you cannot be sure it is actually *seeing* you! Will you:

Run for the other door?	Turn to **237**
Attempt to speak with the creature?	Turn to **357**
Move slowly towards the boxes in the corner?	Turn to **200**

258

None of your offerings are of any particular interest to these creatures, who are much more interested in you than your gifts. You try to impress them with an Illusion Spell, creating a colourful rainbow across the centre of the room. They are fascinated and allow you to pass through to the far door – turn to **140**. If you do not have an Illusion Spell, you must use one of your other Spells to impress them. If you have no other Spells, you must approach them – turn to **366**.

259

Dismayed, she watches as you float into the air above her. She spins herself frantically, trying to suck you down, but you are out of reach. You taunt her with a smile and a wave and float over towards the Black Tower, setting yourself down outside the main entrance. Turn to **218**.

260

After some struggling, the box opens. Inside is a silver key. Will you:

Try to use the key on the second box?	Turn to **34**
Try to use the key on the third box?	Turn to **299**
Take the key and make for the exit door?	Turn to **237**

261

The Ape-Dog asks to see your herbs. Luckily, you grabbed a few handfuls of weeds on your way and you show them. Cocking its head to one side, the creature eyes you suspiciously. It asks you for the name of the guard you have come to treat – something you hadn't planned on! You quickly think of a name to bluff the creature with:

Kylltrog	Turn to **81**
Pincus	Turn to **175**
Blag	Turn to **394**

262

As you cast the spell, an identical Gark, similarly armed, appears before you. At your command, the battle starts:

GARK   *SKILL 7*   *STAMINA 11*

If your creation loses, you will have to finish the battle to the death on your own with your sword. If either you or your Gark defeat the creature, turn to **180**.

263

Calacorms are reliable and contented creatures. They are large reptilian beasts, with grey skin, long tails and two heads, which chatter at each other incessantly. They want for little, having no great ambitions in life beyond their jobs, their food (they live on dead snakes) and their home comforts. Rather out of character with their placid nature is their great delight in the screams and pain of torture and, strangely enough, these creatures are for some reason scared to death by mice, in spite of their huge size. Turn to **326**.

264

Your great muscles flex and grip your sword hilt tightly. You stand and face the RHINO-MAN ready for battle. In view of your extra strength, you may roll one of the dice again when rolling for your *Attack Strength* (i.e. your *Attack Strength* will be your *SKILL* score plus the roll of three dice instead of the normal two):

RHINO-MAN　　　　　　*SKILL 8*　　　　　　*STAMINA 9*

If you win, you may enter the Black Tower, turn to **177**.

265

You are in a short corridor, which ends at a large wooden door ahead. You try the handle and the door opens into a large room. Turn to **169**.

266

He is not interested in your chat, or your stories, and questions your authority to be there. Without warning, he turns into a Snake, hissing at you, and slithers across the floor towards you. Meanwhile, the Dog Head on the wall has detached itself and is now floating through the air towards you. Will you use a Spell against them (turn to **310**) or search through your backpack for something to use (turn to **54**)?

267

As you grasp the chalice, the liquid turns green, then a dirty brown in front of your eyes. It smells putrid, but you take a sip. With a grimace you spit it out – you are drinking muddy water! You leave the chamber and head for the Citadel. Turn to **156**, and lose one *LUCK* point.

268

As you hit the door, the wood cracks a little but does not give. You try it again and this time the wood splits down the middle. You break your way through into the room behind it. Turn to **210**.

269

The two men are dirty and unkempt. As you approach you can hear them arguing loudly about the price of a dagger. The taller of the two is obviously trying to sell the dagger to the other. He argues that the dagger is enchanted and is worth more than the other is willing to pay for it. As you come closer, he grabs you by the arm and asks you for your opinion on the price of the weapon. What will you say:

5 Gold Pieces?   Turn to **205**
8 Gold Pieces?   Turn to **186**
10 Gold Pieces?   Turn to **225**

270

You may take either the door on the left or the right. If you take the door on the left, turn to **185**. If you want to try the other door, turn to **23**.

271

You grasp his hand and introduce yourself – and cry out as the nerves down your arm go numb! O'Seamus bursts out laughing. Lose 1 *SKILL* point, as you were using your sword arm. You are becoming angry, but the little man continues to shake your hand and laugh. A laugh comes from behind you and you look round to see him floating in the air, grinning. But you are still shaking his hand in front of you ... or are you? In fact, you now realize you are frantically shaking hands with a stuffed dummy which is flopping around on the end of your arm as you shake it. You throw it to the ground – but it is stuck to your hand! The situation is ludicrous, and you are becoming very angry. 'Just a little joke,' says the Leprechaun, who snaps his ringers. The dummy disappears. 'Now, what can I do for you?' Will you ask him the way onwards (turn to **348**), or draw your sword (turn to **131**)?

272

You go through his pockets and find 8 Gold Pieces. The Pocket Myriad has, unfortunately, been damaged in the fight, but you may be able to find some use for it and may take it with you. Now you may either investigate the Wine Cellar (turn to **242**), or press on through it to the door at the far end of the room (turn to **95**).

273

Is the password:

Scimitar?	Turn to **371**
Ganjees?	Turn to **255**
Kraken?	Turn to **49**

274

The armoury cupboard is locked, but can easily be smashed. Inside are various swords and pikes. Will you smash the lock and choose a weapon (turn to **353**), or rummage through your backpack for an artefact to use (turn to **277**)?

275

You recognize the device as a Pocket Myriad, an enchanted gadget which can become any one of a number of weapons or useful artefacts. You both close for battle. You may fight him with your sword:

BLACK ELF   *SKILL 8*   *STAMINA 4*

Or you may cast a Spell. If you cast a Weakness Spell, his *SKILL* is reduced to 5. If you cast a Creature Copy Spell, an identical Black Elf with a Pocket Myriad will fight the Elf (resolve the battle between them and if the original Black Elf wins, you must finish him off yourself). If you wish to cast an Illusion Spell, turn to **399**. If you fight him and win, turn to **272**.

276

You fall to the bottom of a deep pit – possibly a filled-in well. You pick yourself up and you appear to be intact. But how are you going to get out? To dig footholes up the sides of the pit with your sword would take far too long. You could cast a Strength Spell to assist you in this (turn to **165**), or you could shout for help (turn to **202**). Which will you choose?

277

You no doubt have collected several artefacts on your way through the Citadel. Do you have any of the following? If so, you may use one now:

A Spider in a Jar   Turn to **330**
A Pocket Myriad   Turn to **315**
Small Berries   Turn to **76**

If you have none of these, turn to **119**.

278

Runestones is a somewhat dangerous game, but the prizes are high. Before the game begins, your Games Master, who is an apprentice sorcerer, casts a Spell on a rock, which will cause it to explode some time later. The players stand in a circle and toss the rock from one to another around the circle. When the rock explodes, the player holding it is out of the game – and winds up with badly burned hands! The remaining players are given another Runestone to toss around again and the game continues until there is only one player left. Onlookers bet on the players but, before they can bet, they must contribute 3 Gold Pieces each to the prize money. In this game you will stand to win 36 Gold Pieces, at the risk of injuring your hands. Having chosen this option, you must play the game at least once, but you may continue to play for as long as you like. If you win, you will claim 36 Gold Pieces for each game you play. If you lose, you must deduct 2 *SKILL* and 4 *STAMINA* points for each game.

Play the game like this: roll one die to see how many other players will join you. Give each player a letter (A, B, C, etc. – you are player A) and write them down on a piece of paper, in a circle. Then throw another die for each player to see who starts with the stone (highest throw starts). Throw two dice for the starting player, who must throw less than 12. Move on to the next player, clockwise round the circle, who must throw less than 11. The third player must throw less than 10, and so on. Move your pencil from letter to letter around the circle to keep track of who has the Runestone. As soon as one player throws higher than the target number, the stone explodes and that player is out. Then start the whole thing again (i.e. the target number goes back to 12), without the loser. Keep on going until just one player remains. If any player throws the same as the target number, the stone explodes in mid air and you must repeat the round.

When you have had enough you may either play Six Pick (turn to **171**), Knifey-Knifey (turn to **365**), or you may leave the gaming room (turn to **31**).

279

You rise into the air. The room continues to shake around you but you can float freely. You may fly to wherever you wish in the room:

To the armoury cupboard?	Turn to **44**
Quickly nip behind the sorcerer?	Turn to **318**
Over to the window?	Turn to **78**
Under the table?	Turn to **335**

280

The creature is savaging you mercilessly and you are powerless to prevent it. Your leg is covered in blood and the pain is sickening. To no avail you struggle with the unseen head. You are in agony. The creature lunges at your neck, and your last memory, before losing consciousness, is of its jaws closing around your throat. Turn to **323**.

281

You open the door into another room and surprise four small creatures sitting on the bare floor. They spring to their feet, shocked at your arrival. Will you:

Draw your sword and make ready for an attack?	Turn to **382**
Tell them you are just passing through?	Turn to **285**
Try to make conversation with them?	Turn to **356**

282

You cast a small fireball directly at the Sewer Snake, which burns through its body cutting it into two halves. Both halves now attack you and are crushing your chest. Lose 2 *STAMINA* points. Trying a different strategy, you create flames which burn in each hand and rub them over the Snake's coils. The creature twitches violently and releases its grip! You find its head and smother it in your flaming hands, burning it to death. Turn to **112**.

283

Without magic, your fate is sealed. You are doomed to spend the rest of your days as a prisoner in the Citadel of Chaos.

You have failed in your mission.

284

You cast the Spell (cross it off your Spell List) and start to rise into the air. The tentacle will not let go and the pain in your leg becomes excruciating. You decide to return to earth before your leg is wrenched from its socket. You will have to either fight it with your sword (turn to **71**), or cast a Fire Spell (turn to **114**).

285

You tell them you mean them no harm, you are just on your way onwards. They sigh with relief. The room is sparsely decorated with bits of foliage and a small fire burns under a hole in the ceiling in one corner. In the wall opposite there are two doors. The little creatures tell you you can make your way onwards through either of these doors. Will you choose the door on the left (turn to **185**), or the door on the right (turn to **23**)?

286

The little creatures squeal and huddle together as you approach. You run them all through with your sword, but they put up no resistance! You feel a little wary at such an easy battle and make for the door at the far end of the room. Turn to **140**.

287

You offer the Jar of Ointment. Something invisible whisks it out of your hand and over to one of the animal heads. Unseen hands unscrew the top and the head sniffs the ointment inside. Turning to you, the head snorts, 'Why this is naught but an alchemist's healing balm! What use have we for this?' The Jar falls to the floor and smashes. You may either:

Offer a Pocket Myriad   Turn to **160**
Offer some Gold Pieces   Turn to **27**
Or beat a hasty exit and try
the other door   Turn to **25**

288

The two creatures advance. The Ape-Dog attacks you first, followed by the Dog-Ape. Will you cast a spell or stand and fight?

You may cast:

A Strength Spell   Turn to **162**
A Levitation Spell   Turn to **86**

Or you may fight them in turn:

	SKILL	STAMINA
APE-DOG	7	4
DOG-APE	6	6

If you kill them both in battle, turn to **32**.

289

What will you take from your backpack?

A Silver Mirror?	Turn to **340**
A Vial of Hogweed Essence?	Turn to **214**
A Jar of Ointment?	Turn to **305**

If you have none of these, return to **304** and choose again.

290

The RHINO-MAN steps forwards and jabs at you with its pike. You leap quickly out of the way. Although it is not wearing armour, its thick hide looks protection enough. You must decide whether to take it on in combat or to use your magic. Will you draw your sword (turn to **325**), or try a spell? You may use:

A Weakness Spell	Turn to **307**
A Levitation Spell	Turn to **70**
A Strength Spell	Turn to **264**

291

'What is that?' demands a ghostly voice. You bargain with them. You will allow them to take the ointment if they will allow you through the room; you have no business with them. A ghostly hand appears from nowhere and tries to snatch the Jar from your hand, but you whip it away quickly. 'It is indeed the Ointment of Healing,' you hear one of the voices say quietly. 'We accept your offer,' says a voice. 'Leave the Jar where you are and leave through this door.' A door in the far corner glows softly. You do not trust them and take the Jar with you to the door. As you open the door you fling the Jar across the room and leave quickly. Turn to **328**.

292

The room is an elegant bed-chamber, plushly decorated with fine lace and a fur carpet. In the centre of the room is a large four-poster bed. Sitting up in the bed, evidently awakened by all the commotion, is a beautiful, sylph-like woman with long dark hair and deep piercing eyes. 'What right have you in here?' she screams at you. With those words her eyes turn blood-red and two jets of liquid fire shoot from them directly at you. Will you:

Create a Shielding Spell to
protect yourself? Turn to **376**
Leave the room quickly and
try the next door? Turn to **64**
Tell her you have a special
gift for her? Turn to **42**

293

In the nick of time, your Spell stops the Trident in mid-flight, horribly close to your neck. It drops to the ground. Turn to **374**.

294

The Gark straightens up, lowers its axe and begins apologizing to you for being asleep at its post. At its insistence you agree not to tell anyone. The creature offers to take your tunic, but you decline its offer and press onwards. Turn to **99**.

295

You concentrate and begin to turn yourself into a Giant Scorpion. The Dwarf and the Goblin stop in their tracks, but the Orc behaves as if nothing has happened. The other two see you sting the Orc with your tail, but the Orc does not flinch and calls the other two on. Seeing that you have done no damage, they shake their heads and look again to see the real you. The Orc tries to grab you. Turn to **213**.

296

The key turns and the door opens. Turn to **292**.

297

You slam the door shut behind you and, above the clanging bell, you can hear the sound of footsteps, running quickly and getting closer. The corridor ahead forks two ways. Will you spring ahead and take the right fork (turn to **2**), or the left fork (turn to **316**) – or will you go back through the door and ring for the butler (turn to **75**)?

298

As your hands close around the chalice, it begins to fizz and foam, spitting at you as you raise it to your lips. Are you sure you want to taste it? If not, turn back to **58** and make another choice – but if you are determined, turn to **141**.

299

The key will not turn, no matter how hard you try. In your frustration, you throw the box on the ground – and it vanishes! You grope around for the invisible box but cannot feel it anywhere. In total despair, you turn towards the door and set off once more towards your goal. Turn to **237**.

300

Throw one die. If you roll a 1, 2 or 3, then this number of knives hit you (each knife does 2 *STAMINA* points' worth of damage). If you roll a 4, 5 or 6, then they miss you. You must prepare to counter-attack either with an Illusion Spell (turn to **244**), or by drawing your sword (turn to **346**).

301

You feel strength surging through your body. You try to wrestle with the head of this creature but its own strength seems also to have increased to match yours. Your leg is now useless and covered in blood. Your strength begins to fade, and as it does so, the creature's jaws close on your throat. Consciousness fades. Turn to **323**.

302

They order you to take a tray of food through a door in the far wall into the Great Hall and leave it on the table, as the Ganjees will soon be down for their supper. They also warn you not to wait for the Ganjees, or you are likely to wind up as the next meal. You take the tray and leave through the far door.

Glad to be out of their repulsive kitchen, you follow a passageway onwards, pause to leave the tray behind, and continue to another door. You try the handle and it opens. Turn to **169**.

303

The Golem advances and you slash at it with your sword. Your sword hits solid rock and clangs noisily. You will have to resolve this battle and deduct 1 *SKILL* point during the fight:

GOLEM   *SKILL 8*   *STAMINA 10*

If you defeat the creature, turn to **147**.

As you enter the room, the creature creaks as its head turns towards you

304

The door opens and you enter the room. It is quite large and is decorated with various carvings. It looks something like an artist's studio and a number of unfinished stone statues line one wall. In the centre of the room, a large stone GARGOYLE is standing on a stone-carved box. As you enter the room, the creature creaks as its head turns towards you. Slowly it comes alive, hopping down off its pedestal. It blocks your way through the room to a door on the far side. What will you do:

Draw your sword and advance?	Turn to **172**
Prepare to cast a Spell?	Turn to **26**
Look through your bag for something to use?	Turn to **289**
Nip out of this room and try the middle door?	Turn to **64**

305

You throw the Jar at the Gargoyle. It smashes but does no damage. The creature swipes out at you and hits you in the chest, knocking you over. Lose 2 *STAMINA* points. You had better leave this room quickly and head along the balcony to the middle door. Turn to **64**.

306

A short distance further on, a door blocks the passageway. In fact, this is only a half-door and is about waist-high to you. A sign by the door points onwards and says 'Players Only'. Will you push open this door (turn to **52**), or turn back and enter the room with the fancy door (turn to **132**)?

307

As you cast the Spell, the creature lunges at you and clips your arm with its pike. Lose 2 *STAMINA* points.

Then the Weakness Spell takes effect. The creature slows down and starts puffing and panting. You draw your sword and advance to finish him off.

RHINO-MAN   *SKILL 4*   *STAMINA 7*

If you defeat him, you may enter the Citadel. Turn to **177**.

308

The handle turns and you step into a dark room. Turn to **257**.

309

You both go through the tall man's pockets. You find 20 Gold Pieces, which you split equally, and you toss up for the dagger; heads you get it, tails he does *(toss a coin for this)*. If you get the dagger, turn to **15**. If not, turn to **245**.

310

Will you use:

A Creature Copy Spell?	Turn to **181**
An Illusion Spell?	Turn to **250**
An E.S.P. Spell?	Turn to **393**

If you have none of these, return to **104** and choose again.

311

You concentrate hard, mumbling your Spell's incantations. One of the old women notices you and shouts to the other two. You cast your Spell – but nothing happens! You glance at the old hags, who are smiling at you. 'We cannot allow you to use magic against our pet,' says one of them. You have wasted a Spell. Cross one (of your choice) off your Spells. Now the Devlin is almost on you and you will have to either dive for cover (turn to **178**), or draw your sword (turn to **61**).

312

You hold up the Mirror. This seems to have little effect on the creature, which continues its advance. One head springs forwards and knocks the mirror from your hands, smashing it on the floor. You try to decide what to do next. Turn to **184**.

313

The fruit is sweet and juicy. You eat one, then another – it tastes delicious! Gain 2 *STAMINA* points. But to your surprise, as you try to clear your throat afterwards, not a sound comes from your mouth. You have eaten a Fruit of Silence. Its peculiar effect is only temporary, but you will not be able to speak properly for some time although you will be able to make yourself understood with difficulty. This means, in effect, that you will not be able to use your magic (the next time a Spells option is given) but after this you will return to normal. You may continue either through the door in the left-hand wall (turn to **13**), or through the door opposite the one you have just come through (turn to **281**).

314

You try to concentrate, creating the illusion that the sorcerer is likewise in a shaking room. The Spell is cast (and you must cross it off your list) but it has no effect; you cannot concentrate fully. Balthus Dire is almost upon you. Turn to **373**.

315

Balthus Dire falls into a state of concentration as you fiddle with your Pocket Myriad. You press one button and a shimmering light comes from it, extending to about sword-length. This is a Sun-Sword and will add 4 points to your *SKILL* when you fight with it! You turn to face the sorcerer, who has been concentrating on a Spell. Turn to **191**.

They move by cartwheeling along at quite a rapid pace

316

The footsteps you heard – which really ought to be called 'handsteps' – belong to three WHEELIES which now roll down the passageway towards you, forcing you back to the door. These creatures are peculiar beasts having, instead of legs, an extra set of hands. They move by cartwheeling along at quite a rapid pace. Their heads – or at least their faces – are set in the centre of their chests. While they are not well-practised at swordsmanship given their awkward means of movement, they are excellent knife-throwers. Grasping knives from their belts as they spin along, they can launch them at a rapid-fire pace, like large Catherine wheels. At the moment, three such knives are speeding their way towards you. You may either use a Shielding Spell to protect you (turn to **220**) or *Test your Luck*. If you opt for the latter and are lucky, turn to **139**. If you are Unlucky, turn to **300**.

317

The paintings are portraits of various Lords and Earls prominent in the Kingdom of Craggen Rock. Behind a chair at the head of the table is a portrait of Balthus Dire himself. He does indeed look a powerful adversary. Add 1 *LUCK* point for the warning of his appearance, but lose 1 *STAMINA* point for the feeling of fear he instils. You may now continue either up the left-hand staircase (turn to **19**), or the right-hand staircase (turn to **197**).

318

The sorcerer is showing signs of mental exhaustion and is slow to react as you stop behind him. You notice he is wearing a gold ring with a large ruby set in it on the index finger of his right hand, which hangs by his side. You may either try to grab the ring from his finger (turn to **381**), draw your sword quickly (turn to **117**), or search through your backpack for an artefact to use (turn to **277**).

319

You concentrate on your arm. It begins to harden and turns the dull metallic colour of iron. The old man's eyes widen as he sees your iron forearm. You wrestle to free yourself but still his teeth keep their grip. Lose 2 *STAMINA* points and cross off your Illusion Spell. Your illusion obviously wasn't convincing enough. You go for your sword. Turn to **333**.

320

You concentrate hard, but try as you might, you receive none of Balthus Dire's thoughts – he is blocking your Spell! You may continue with an Illusion Spell (turn to **332**), a Weakness Spell (turn to **113**), or you may draw your sword to attack him (turn to **351**).

321

Cautiously, and keeping well out of sight, you creep through the darkness around the edge of the courtyard. There are two groups of creatures in front of you. To the right, you can see two human-like figures talking under a torch fastened to the wall. To the left, a group of four creatures, of varying shapes and sizes, are sitting around a fire, eating. Will you approach the two by the torch (turn to **269**), or the group around the fire (turn to **339**)?

322

What will you pull from your backpack?

A Spider in a Jar?	Turn to **39**
A Charmed Amulet?	Turn to **168**
A Jar of Ointment?	Turn to **291**

If you have none of these, you will have to draw your sword and face them (turn to **248**).

323

You awake and look around. As your memory returns, you are amazed that you *can* see! Your leg feels tender, but is uninjured! You hear a small chuckle coming from above you and suddenly the whole thing makes sense...

Floating above you is O'Seamus, now laughing loudly.

The whole thing has been one big practical joke! You are enraged and leap to your feet, but as you glare at the funny little man rolling about in the air in hysterics, you can't help but see the funny side too. You chuckle, then giggle, then laugh loudly. For some time the two of you roar with laughter until tears stream down your faces.

When you are both able to control yourselves, you eventually settle down to chat. He is a pleasant little man. Before you leave, he says, 'Indeed you are a good sport. Your way ahead is fraught with danger, though. But perhaps these will help you.' With a wave of his hand, a sword and a plate appear on the table. The sword is a magic battlesword and will add 1 point to the dice roll when throwing for your *Attack Strength*. The plate is, in fact, a Silver Mirror of fine workmanship. You may take these with you, but you will have to leave your old sword behind. Leave the room through either:

The brass-handled door   Turn to **386**
The copper-handled door   Turn to **144**
The bronze-handled door   Turn to **338**

324

'You cannot hide from me!' he cries. This is indeed true, and you realize you could be in some danger while you cannot see him. Turn to **369**.

325

The creature is somewhat bulky and clumsy, snorting furiously as you avoid his blows. You draw your sword and fight:

RHINO-MAN   *SKILL 8*   *STAMINA 9*

If you defeat him, you may enter the Citadel. Turn to **177**.

326

You replace the book. Will you continue browsing through the books (turn to **84**), or will you leave through the door at the far end, behind the librarian (turn to **31**)?

327

They take your Pocket Myriad and play with it gleefully. While they are suitably distracted, you can creep past them to the door on the far side of the room. Turn to **366**. Cross your gift off your Equipment List.

A huge, six-headed hydra snakes towards you

328

You close the door behind you and find yourself at the foot of yet another staircase, spiralling up into the tower. Climbing the stairs, you arrive at another balcony where a single door is the only way onwards. Trying the door, it opens easily. But, as you push the door, a loud hissing noise comes from within. You step inside and turn cold as a huge, six-headed HYDRA snakes towards you over the bodies of its previous victims! Its six serpent-like heads dart at you, with vicious pointed teeth. You cower into the corner. What will you do:

Draw your sword and fight the creature?	Turn to **67**
Use a Creature Copy Spell?	Turn to **143**
Use something from your backpack?	Turn to **226**

329

You concentrate on her mind and you are shocked to find that she is not alive, as she seems, but has been dead for many years. Ever since a raging fire – a curse put on her by Balthus Dire himself for failing to launder his robes in time for an important meeting – burned her and her children to death, her ghostly body has been doomed to wash clothes for eternity. She is indeed a miserable wretch. You now notice that she is growing angry and suspicious with your presence. She is chanting something under her breath. Will you attempt to talk to her (turn to **21**), or will you try to move quickly on past her along the path (turn to **221**)?

330

The sorcerer shrieks in horror as you pull out the Jar. Sensing that this little creature may be a valuable ally, you open the Jar and release it. The sorcerer's expression changes to a sly smile and, as you watch, the little Spider-Man advances not towards Balthus Dire, but towards you! You must fight it:

SPIDER-MAN   *SKILL 7*   *STAMINA 5*

As soon as the creature inflicts its first wound on you, turn to **208**. If you defeat it without injury, turn to **119**.

331

The Snapperfish's sharp teeth catch your face and nose as you try to pull back. Lose 1 *SKILL* and 3 *STAMINA* points as you nurse your bloody face. The three old hags shuffle round the kettle to you and bundle you off towards the door at the far end of the kitchen. Shoving you through the door, they taunt and insult you, closing the door behind you. Turn to **265**.

332

Balthus Dire's jaw drops as a transformation takes place in front of his eyes. Your body grows in size and strength. Your skin turns a deep red and horns crack through the tight skin on your forehead. Your teeth are sharp black spikes and your tongue, now forked, hisses menacingly at him. You now stand before him as a FIRE DEMON and you grab the Trident from the ground as a weapon. The sorcerer turns away from you in horror. You may either spring across the table at him (turn to **80**), or command him to call off his plans of conquest and surrender to you (turn to **48**).

333

You draw your sword and prepare to chop him with it. He glances up at you with a look that leads you to believe that he is not completely in control of his own actions. With pity, you crack him on the head with your sword hilt, causing him to howl and release his grip. You leave him moaning on the ground, nursing his head. Lose another 2 *STAMINA* points for the damage he has done to your arm and press onwards. Turn to **14**.

334

You take a couple of sips. Not bad! You take a mouthful but as you do so, you wonder why the Elf is chuckling. Suddenly he asks whether you really are a guest. Although your mind is confirming that you are indeed a visitor, your voice is telling him that you are not; you have come to put an end to Balthus Dire's plans of conquest! You curse as you realize that the wine must be spiked with a Truth Serum. The Black Elf now knows of your mission and must be prevented from telling others. You draw your sword and, as you do so, he pulls a small metallic device from the pouch tied around his waist. With a touch, it turns into a saw-edged weapon. Turn to **275**.

335

Fixed under the table is a secret drawer, slightly ajar, and poking out of the drawer is a scroll of parchment. You grab the scroll and thrust it into your tunic. But you can hear Balthus murmuring under his breath. A Spell!

But what will this one be? And what can you do about it? Suddenly he is running around the table, touching each side as he goes. At his touch, the table responds with a cracking noise. Turn to **342**.

336

Resolve your battle with the creature:

GARK	*SKILL 7*	*STAMINA 11*

After four *Attack Rounds* you may *Escape* through one of the doors at the far end of the room (turn to **99**), otherwise you may continue and fight to the death. If you do so and win, turn to **180**.

337

The sorcerer is indeed as great a swordsman as he is a wizard. Resolve your battle:

BALTHUS DIRE	*SKILL 12*	*STAMINA 19*

If you have managed to steal the sorcerer's ring, you may deduct 2 points from his *SKILL,* as he was wearing a Ring of Swordsmanship.

If you defeat Balthus Dire, turn to **400**.

*As you approach they stop and turn round to
look at you with unwelcoming faces*

338

The door opens into a passageway. You follow the passageway onwards for some time and it twists and turns through the rock. You pass another passageway joining from the right and carry straight on. Eventually the path widens out. Turn to **90**.

339

A motley crew sit around the fire. A warty-faced Orc is handing out scraggy chunks of half-cooked meat to the others. A snarling Dwarf with green skin is complaining about the size of his piece, while two scruffy Goblins – a man and a woman – are cuddling each other. They giggle and laugh, and every so often she slaps his ugly face causing more merriment. As you approach they stop and turn round to look at you with unwelcoming faces. They sneer at your neat appearance and the female Goblin whispers some comment to her mate. In front of the Dwarf you can see an open box. You can just make out a vial of liquid within it. Will you:

Sit down with them around the fire?	Turn to **134**
Ask them whether you may join them?	Turn to **149**

340

You hold up the mirror, but the creature merely swings at it and smashes it into pieces. You had better leave the room quickly and try the middle door on the balcony. Turn to **64**.

341

You cast the Spell around yourself and advance. Four or five arrows sing towards you but stop in the air a metre before they reach you, dropping harmlessly to the ground. You reach the monument. Remember to cross the Shielding Spell off your list. Turn to **209**.

342

The sorcerer stands back from the table and laughs. 'Now I have you, peasant!' he gloats. Cautiously, you step out from beneath the table. That is, you *try* to step out. But you cannot reach out further than the table's edge. He has created invisible walls which now trap you underneath! Try as you might, you cannot break through his barriers.

You are now his prisoner. You have failed in your mission...

343

A little further along the passage, you arrive at another fork where you may go either left (turn to **55**), or right (turn to **249**).

344

You follow the stairs downwards. The air is cool and stagnant. At the foot of the stairs is a door. Will you try the door (turn to **7**), or climb the stairs again and go up to the door to the ground floor (turn to **5**)?

345

The creature groans as the Spell takes effect. Its enormous weight is now a great burden to it. It shambles towards you still, but you are able to sidestep it and head for the door on the far side of the room. Turn to **140**.

346

As the Wheelies see you draw your sword, they stop and chatter excitedly. One of them – evidently the leader – sends the smallest one back up the passage (presumably to fetch help). The other two draw knives and roll slowly towards you. Resolve this battle (fight each in turn):

	SKILL	STAMINA
First WHEELIE	7	6
Second WHEELIE	6	5

If you win you may take either the left-hand passage (turn to **243**), or the right-hand passage (turn to **2**).

347

The Gorgon sees the mirror and shrieks. You chance a look at the creature, your gaze rising upwards from its feet. But the Gorgon has disappeared and instead Balthus Dire stands once more before you. Turn to **12**.

348

'Oh, I shouldn't go *this* way,' says O'Seamus. 'These are not pleasant parts.' These three doors are the only ways onward. Two of them are *very* dangerous and the other is very smelly. On the opposite side of the room are three doors. One has a brass handle, one has a copper handle and one has a bronze handle. Which will you choose:

The brass-handled door?	Turn to **207**
The copper-handled door?	Turn to **22**
The bronze-handled door?	Turn to **354**
Or will you ask his advice?	Turn to **68**

A replica of Balthus Dire materializes in front of you. Dire himself raises an eyebrow. 'Attack! you command the duplicate, who turns towards the centre of the room and advances. Two metres from the sorcerer, it stops and clutches its head. It looks up from its hands, turns and comes towards *you*! The sorcerer laughs. "Two can play at this game!' says Dire. You concentrate and will the replica back towards Dire. Eventually it ceases its approach and turns back as you command. For some moments this goes on, and you realize that you both have the power to command this creature, but only within a certain range. Backwards and forwards it goes, until the Spell begins to wear off. It gradually fades from view. The concentration has been somewhat strenuous for you. You look up to see Balthus Dire holding his hands in the air and then bring them down hard on the table. What magic is he using now? Turn to **157**.

350

You try a simple ploy to get rid of her, hoping that she is not too intelligent. Looking into the shadows, you claim to see another similar creature. She claims you are mistaken, but you are convincing. She nips off to investigate, allowing you to rush to the Citadel entrance. Turn to **218**.

351

As you advance with your sword drawn, the sorcerer pulls a scimitar from his belt. 'Yes,' he gloats, 'I will take great delight in finishing this off with weapons!' And with those words he leaps over the table towards you. The battle to follow will be a fight to the death:

BALTHUS DIRE   *SKILL 12*   *STAMINA 19*

If you slay the sorcerer, turn to **400**.

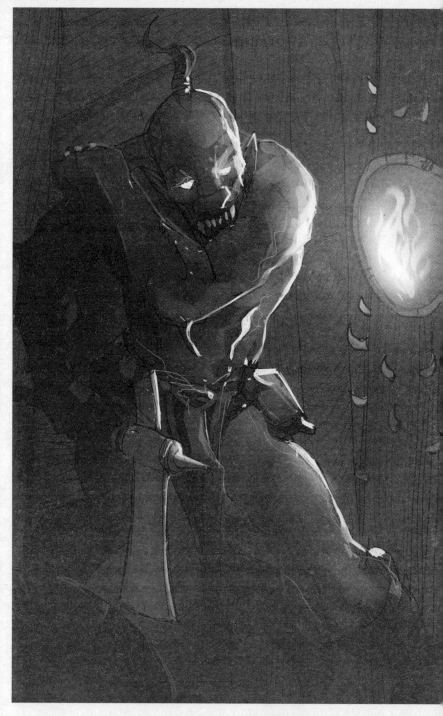

One eye opens, then another and, seeing you, it springs to its feet

352

You tiptoe into the room. The room is gloomy and the air is damp. A crude wooden post is nailed to one wall with several hooks on it. There are two doors in the far wall leading onwards. On the post, hanging on the wall, is a makeshift mirror but as your torch lights up the mirror, its reflection is thrown across the eyes of the sleeping giant, who grunts and stirs. One eye opens, then another and, seeing you, it springs to its feet! It grabs an axe, which it was using as a pillow, and quickly undoes the leather sheath to reveal a sharp bronze head. This giant creature is a GARK! Large and brutish, Garks are half-Goblin, half-Giant, bred by master sorcerers for their aggressive character. Although somewhat stupid, they are rather tough beasts with a war-like nature. Will you:

Make a dash for the doors?	Turn to **203**
Draw your sword, ready for a fight?	Turn to **16**
Apologize for disturbing the creature?	Turn to **216**
Prepare to use a Spell?	Turn to **11**

353

Many deadly weapons are inside the cabinet, but a blue-honed sword takes your eye. Balthus Dire sees you take this sword and flies into a rage. 'Do not touch that weapon!' he screams. But he is too late; you have it in your hands. 'So be it,' he says, sliding a scimitar from his own belt and advancing towards you. The battle to follow will, you realize, be a fight to the death.

BALTHUS DIRE   *SKILL* 12   *STAMINA* 19.

Your new weapon is an enchanted sword which will add two points to your dice roll when determining your *Attack Strength*.

If you win, turn to **400**.

354

You open the door and step into another room, glad to have left the annoying little creature behind. Turn to **188**.

355

If you will not (or cannot) use your magic, you will have to rely on your sword. Draw your sword and turn to **351**.

They are somewhat relieved that you mean them no harm, and settle back on to the floor, inviting you to join them. The room is small and plain and bits of greenery have been mounted on the walls, presumably for decoration, although the leaves are now wilted and long-dead. A small fire burns in one corner, under a hole in the ceiling. Two doors are in the wall opposite you; one on the left, the other on the right. You sit down for a chat. You discover that these small, skinny creatures call themselves SCOUTS and they are indeed a likeable lot, joking and laughing with you. You decide not to risk telling them too much of your mission, but you ask general questions about the place. Balthus Dire is the master of the house and spends most of his time high up in the Citadel. His ladywife is a beautiful sorceress who is very vain and who enjoys the things that money and power can buy. There are many evil creatures within the Citadel, but you must be particularly careful of the Ganjees, who roam the Tower at night. Eventually you get up, thank them for the chat and prepare to press on. You may add 2 *STAMINA* and 1 *LUCK* point for the rest and information you have gained. The Scouts also offer to do a good deed for you before you go, as they have also enjoyed your company. You may either:

Take them up on their offer	Turn to **146**
Decide not to risk it and leave through the door on the left	Turn to **185**
Leave through the door on the right	Turn to **23**

357

The creature is apparently deaf-mute. You hail it in all the languages you know, but it continues to stand silently. You make a move towards the centre of the room. Turn to **200**.

358

Unfortunately, you are not in much of a position to issue idle threats. The sorcerer merely laughs loudly and tightens his hold. He tells you to reconsider, or your death is certain. Will you continue to refuse his offer, not wishing to turn traitor to your countrymen (turn to **148**), or will you agree to come under his command (turn to **256**)?

359

You try to duck, but cannot avoid the full impact of the missile, which hits you on the forehead and splatters all over your face. You brace yourself, waiting perhaps for an acidic reaction to take place, but the mushy liquid merely drips off your face on to the ground. Cautiously you test it, first with your finger, then with your tongue. You have just been hit by a ripe tomato! You turn to face the sleeping figure once more. Turn to **29**.

360

You cast another Spell. Your partially-formed Hydra grows a little more, but is still not complete. You will need one more Creature Copy Spell to form a whole creature. If you wish to cast this third Spell, do so and let the Hydras fight to the death:

HYDRA　　　　　　*SKILL 10*　　　　　*STAMINA 17*

If your creation wins, turn to **229**. If your creature loses, or if you did not have enough Spells to complete the creation, you must decide what to do next (turn to **184**).

361

Again the door opens but as you open it, you hear the deafening clanging of an alarm bell! *Test your Luck.* If you are Lucky, turn to **297**. If you are Unlucky, turn to **126**.

Fluttering around the altar are three winged gremlin-type creatures

362

The door opens and the small room inside is lit by candlelight. Cautiously you look inside to see a strange sight. On a stone altar in the middle of the chamber are three silver chalices, each containing a different-coloured liquid; one clear, one red and one milky. Fluttering around the altar are three small winged gremlin-type creatures, all chirping excitedly. Every so often one lands on the altar and takes a sip of the milky liquid. The open door creaks on its hinges and startles them. They whirl round to see you and become very excited. You may either enter the chamber (turn to **58**), or close the door quickly and press onwards towards the Citadel (turn to **156**).

363

Along the balcony are 3 doors. Will you try:

The door to the left?	Turn to **228**
The door in the centre?	Turn to **64**
The door to the right?	Turn to **304**

364

As your Spell takes effect, you see a small mouse run towards the table. You curse as you realize that the Spell cannot have worked properly. But hope returns as one of the Calacorm's heads sees the mouse and looks horrified! The other head suddenly notices it, and both throats shriek together! The creature jumps up on to the table, and the Calacorm screams in terror as the harmless little mouse approaches, sniffing fastidiously at the ground on the way. You let the Calacorm suffer for some moments and then call out that you will get rid of the mouse for him, if he will release you. He agrees quickly and throws you the keys. You let yourself out, grab your sword which was leaning against the wall and set off down the passageway. A safe distance away, you break your Spell and the mouse disappears. Turn to **174**.

365

You have chosen a deadly gambling game which is outlawed in most kingdoms. Since you have chosen to play, you must play at least one game, but you may play more if you wish. Your Games Master is an apprentice sorcerer and he has selected a choice of prizes for you. If you survive, you may claim either: two extra Spells (which you may choose from the list at the beginning of the book), 50 Gold Pieces, or an Enchanted Breastplate (which will allow you to deduct 2 points from a creature's dice roll when throwing for its *Attack Strength*).

The game is played like this: six daggers lie on a table. One is a real weapon while the other five have spring-loaded blades and will do you no harm. You are playing the game against one of the other creatures in the room and only one of you will survive. In turn, you must select one of the daggers and stab yourself in the chest with it. If the dagger is real, death is certain. If it is a dummy, it must be returned to the table to be shuffled back in with the other five.

The game continues until one of you selects the real dagger and stabs yourself through the heart, whereupon the survivor can claim the prize. Your opponent will make the first selection. Throw one die for him. Then do the same for yourself. As soon as one of you rolls a 6, the real dagger has been chosen. If this is you, you will have killed yourself!

Now knowing the rules of the game, you can only get out of playing at least once by casting an Illusion Spell (turn to **9**). Otherwise you must play. After you have played, you may either play Six Pick (turn to **171**), Runestones (turn to **278**), or you may bid your 'friends' farewell and leave the room (turn to **31**).

366

As you stride past them, the little creatures watch you silently. They seem merely to find you interesting. You feel that something is not quite right here. Turn to **140**.

367

Some way along the passage, you arrive at a four-way junction. You take a path to the north, which eventually leads you to a large wooden door. You can hear nothing by listening at the keyhole. Will you try to open the door slowly and quietly (turn to **308**), or charge the door down (turn to **121**)?

368

You go through both their pockets and find 28 Gold Pieces, which you take with you. As you are about to press on, you remember the dagger – the source of the argument – and pick it up. Turn to **15**.

369

You must see what he is doing. As you try to peek around the curtain, you feel it flapping around you as if in a wind – although no wind is blowing. The curtain is tightening itself around you. You struggle, but the heavy drape is engulfing you. It is around your throat and head, and you are gasping for breath. Still you struggle on, but to no avail. You begin to feel faint, knowing that once you lose consciousness, the battle will be his. But there is nothing you can do. Your world goes black. . .

You have failed in your mission.

370

The box is solidly made and you cannot break the lock with your hands. You draw your sword to try to hack it off and, as you do so, the box falls on your shin, causing a nasty cut. Deduct 2 *STAMINA* points. Your sword will not break the lock. Will you:

Try to open the first box?	Turn to **260**
Try to open the second box?	Turn to **129**
Forget the boxes and press onwards?	Turn to **237**

371

The creature grunts and opens the door to let you in. Turn to **177**.

372

As you cast your Shielding Spell, a bottle hits you on the shoulder. You feel nothing. Something is not quite right, and you try to cancel your Spell. Unfortunately it has already been cast and you can see the bottles smashing into the magic shield you have created. The bottle which has hit you has disappeared. You curse as you realize that the wine you just tasted must have had some hallucinatory properties and you are imagining the bottle attack. As this idea dawns on you, the bottles cease pelting you. You blink and look again. All the bottles are in place on their racks as normal! You decide to press onwards. Turn to **95**.

373

Balthus Dire kneels down beside you. He grabs your wrists with one hand and you can feel his great physical power, matching his obvious powers of sorcery. 'Peasant,' he says, 'you are indeed a worthy adversary. Your power exceeds that of most wizards. It is a shame to let such talent go to waste. I may kill you now, or I can offer another option. Join with me in my plan to conquer the Vale of Willow. It shall be yours to govern when we succeed. What say you?'

What is your reply?

'Never. I will not turn against
my countryfolk!'   Turn to **148**
'I accept your offer.' (You plan to outwit
him when he releases you.)   Turn to **256**
'Balthus Dire, you are evil! I am
not defeated yet!' (You plan to cast
another Spell at him.)   Turn to **358**

*Leaning against the table, with his eyes
fixed on you, is Balthus Dire himself*

As you compose yourself after your fright, you glance around the room. It is obviously some sort of Military Headquarters. Scrolls with strategic maps hang from the walls, as do portraits of past generals. A bookcase in one corner holds hundreds of leather-bound volumes. Ornate drapes are drawn across a large window. A cabinet along one wall holds pikes and swords of a variety of deadly shapes and sizes. In the centre of the room is a model landscape which you recognize as the Vale of Willow. Armies of miniature troops are positioned on the model. This must be the invasion plan!

Leaning against the table, with eyes fixed on you, is Balthus Dire himself! His very stature is formidable. Well over two metres tall, he is built like an ox, with broad shoulders and muscular arms. In his battle tunic of leather with wide, studded wristbands, he looks more a soldier than the demi-sorcerer he really is.

'Impudent peasant!' he growls, 'Do you think you are any match for Balthus Dire?' With these words he snaps his fingers and you hear a grunting from behind. You swing round to see a grotesque creature shambling towards you. Its hairy body has four arms, each ending in vicious-looking hooks. As it approaches, it slashes the air in front of it. 'Why, I'll wager you are not even a match for a CLAWBEAST!' laughs Dire. Will you:

Draw your sword to defend yourself?	Turn to **30**
Cast a Shielding Spell?	Turn to **109**
Cast a Weakness Spell?	Turn to **158**

375

He indicates a book on the shelf which is an alphabetical listing of all sorts of creatures. Will you turn to the section on:

Calacorms?	Turn to **263**
Miks?	Turn to **135**
Ganjees?	Turn to **63**

376

You cast your Shielding Spell. Alas and alack, this Spell is ineffective against magical weapons! The jets of fire sear straight through your shield and burn into your own eyes. Screaming in pain you drop to the floor. The curtain of death drops over you.

You have failed in your mission.

377

You pick yourself up and concentrate. What will your next attack be?

An Illusion Spell?	Turn to **332**
A Weakness Spell?	Turn to **113**
An E.S.P. Spell?	Turn to **320**
None of these?	Turn to **355**

378

You take a few steps forwards and another arrow narrowly misses your foot. A few more steps and an arrow rips through your tunic, grazing your forearm. You can still see no-one at all, nor can you see where the arrows are coming from. After another few steps, another arrow appears, but this one pierces your calf. You cry out loud – and you must lose 4 *STAMINA* points – but you are almost at the monument, which will provide shelter. You leap forward and duck behind it until the arrows cease. Turn to **209**.

379

You release the rope and float into the air. Dropping back on to the ground on the rim of the trench, you curse at the fiendish trap that had been laid for greedy adventurers like yourself. You move on to the door opposite your entrance and try the handle. Turn to **206**.

380

As you sit down they rise to their feet. The Dwarf picks up a club and springs at you, while the Goblin and the Orc grab swords. The Goblin's mistress gives a cry and jumps out of the way, retreating back into the darkness. Turn to **213**.

381

Test your Luck. If you are Lucky, the ring slides off his finger and you now hold it in your hand. If you are Unlucky, the ring sticks and does not come free. Your snatch fires Balthus Dire into action and he turns on you with his sword. Turn to **337**.

382

They rush round the floor in panic, bumping into each other and crying, 'Oh my, oh dear, this stranger looks nasty, where are our weapons?' You laugh at their disorder and put away your sword. They calm down and stare at you. You may either press onwards (turn to **285**), or talk to them (turn to **356**).

383

The old man's strength begins to return as the Stamina Spell takes effect (deduct this spell from your Spells). He tells you he was beaten about the head by cruel Ganjees, who delight in thuggery. You bring the conversation round to the Citadel itself. Suddenly, for no apparent reason, a stab of pain from within grips him. His eyes narrow to slits and he throws himself forward, sinking his teeth – sharp teeth at that – into your arm. Deduct 2 *STAMINA* points. Will you beat him off with your sword (turn to **333**), or use a Magic Spell to free yourself (turn to **189**)?

384

You fiddle with the gadget and suddenly a long, thin line unwinds itself from the shaft. You decide to try to snare the creature's heads with the line, which has a hook on one end. You cast the line at the creature. Throw one die. If you throw a 5 or 6, turn to **252**. If you throw a 1, 2, 3 or 4, turn to **107**.

385

They clap you on the back and welcome you in. A dark-skinned, wiry creature thrusts a mug of grog into your hand. You drink the ale down in one. Another mug comes. Add 2 *STAMINA* points, as the ale is quite refreshing. Then they invite you to join in their games. Will you play:

Knifey-Knifey?	Turn to **365**
Runestones?	Turn to **278**
Six Pick?	Turn to **171**

386

Outside the door, the passage slopes downwards and you follow it for several minutes. You notice an unpleasant smell which gets stronger and stronger as you go. Eventually you come to an opening.

Looking through it, holding your nose, you can see a large open sewer flowing across the passageway. A rope hangs down from the ceiling. Will you wade across the sewer (turn to **204**), or try to grab the rope and swing across (turn to **108**)?

387

At the mention of a Silver Mirror, she rises, holds up her hands, and commands her Ghosts to stop. You give her the Mirror and she bids you on your way. You are lucky to be alive. Turn to **6**.

His whole body strains with effort. Several moments later he regains his composure and once again looks at you. 'Weakness!' he mocks, 'Surely you don't think *I* could be defeated with a mere Weakness Spell.' He has obviously managed to fight it off and now prepares to launch a counterattack. Turn to **157**.

As you approach the spit, one of the old women throws some powder on to the fire, and the three of them step back, cackling. You are on your guard. As you watch, the fire begins to roar and the flames grow menacingly. Suddenly, several of the flames spring from the fire and take the shape of a DEVLIN, a Dwarf-sized creature, made of fire itself! The three hags point towards you and the Devlin advances.

Will you:

Draw your sword and prepare to fight it?	Turn to **61**
Look for cover?	Turn to **178**
Prepare a Spell?	Turn to **311**

390

She begins to torment you, blowing you off your feet each time you rise. *Test your Luck.* If you are Lucky, turn to **350**. If you are Unlucky, turn to **122**.

391

The Gark takes your 3 Gold Pieces, puts them into a pouch around its waist and shows you onwards to the doors. It asks you whether you would like to go to the Library (right-hand door) or the Games Room (left-hand door). Turn to **99**.

392

The key turns and the door opens. Turn to **196**.

393

You cast your Spell and concentrate on the three changing creatures. Images flash before you. As you fit them together, you realize these creatures are MIKS, and are able to transform themselves into anyone, or anything, they wish. They are thinking of you and are not the least bit worried by your presence – more likely they see you as sport. Every so often, though, they are thinking of gold and their emotions indicate a great greed. Perhaps this will be your passport to safety. If you have any Gold Pieces, turn to **27**. If you have no gold, you had better leave the room quickly and try the other door. Turn to **25**.

394

The creatures look at each other as if the name sounds familiar but they can't quite place it. You quickly add that he is on the first floor watch. They shrug and eventually decide you may be telling the truth. The Ape-Dog summons the gatekeeper who eventually appears to let you in. Turn to **251**.

395

You cast your Spell and concentrate, creating the illusion that you are a powerful sorcerer and you are becoming tired of their pranks. But nothing happens! Again a mocking laugh comes at you from all sides. 'We are magical creatures ourselves,' says a voice, 'though not such amateurs as you!' Suddenly you feel a blow in the middle of your back which knocks you into the middle of the room. Lose 2 *STAMINA* points. Will you fumble in your backpack for something to use (turn to **322**), or draw your sword (turn to **248**)? If you have not yet tried a Fire Spell on them you may do so (turn to **85**).

396

Turn to **183**.

397

This is not much of a meal, but you were hungry and thirsty and this offering restores 2 *STAMINA* points. Now you may either call out the Calacorm (turn to **69**), or choose a Spell to try to get you out of this situation (turn to **193**).

398

You cast the spell and your strength returns to enable you to finish off the steps. As you reach the top the effects wear off once more. You may now set off along the wall towards the Black Tower. Turn to **79**.

399

You cast the Spell. The Elf approaches and, as he does so, the Pocket Myriad disappears from his hand! He stands before you, apparently defenceless, nervously deciding whether to fight on or run. You can nip in quickly and cut him down:

BLACK ELF   *SKILL 4*   *STAMINA 4*

If you win, turn to **272**.

400

Balthus Dire, lying at your feet, is dead. Your mission has been completed! The Vale of Willow is safe from attack – for the time being at least.

To make sure his plan is destroyed, you take the drapes from the window and spread them across the table on which his battle plan is laid out. Taking a candle, you set fire to the rich curtains. As the flames lick the table you consider your own escape. Do you have a Levitation Spell left? If so, you may cast it and float out through the window to the safety of the ground below. If not, then you will need to recall your reserves of skill and cunning to avoid the guards and dangers of the Citadel on your escape. But that is another story...

HOW TO FIGHT
THE CREATURES OF
THE CITADEL OF CHAOS

SKILL, STAMINA AND LUCK

To determine your *initial SKILL, STAMINA* and *LUCK* scores:

- Roll one die. Add 6 to this number and enter this total in the *SKILL* box on the Adventure Sheet.

- Roll both dice. Add 12 to the number rolled and enter this total in the *STAMINA* box.

- Roll one die, add 6 to this number and enter this total in the *LUCK* box.

SKILL reflects your swordsmanship and fighting expertise; the higher the better. *STAMINA* represents your strength; the higher your *STAMINA*, the longer you will survive. *LUCK* represents how lucky a person you are. Luck – and magic – are facts of life in the fantasy world you are about to explore.

SKILL, *STAMINA* and *LUCK* scores change constantly

during an adventure, so keep an eraser handy. You must keep an accurate record of these scores. But never rub out your *initial scores*. Although you may receive additional *SKILL*, *STAMINA* and *LUCK* points, these totals may never exceed your *initial* scores, except on very rare occasions, when instructed on a particular page.

BATTLES

When you are told to fight a creature, you must resolve the battle as described below. First record the creature's *SKILL* and *STAMINA* scores (as given on the page) in an empty *Monster Encounter Box* on your Adventure Sheet. The sequence of combat is then:

1. Roll the two dice for the creature. Add its *SKILL* score. This total is **its** Attack Strength.

2. Roll the two dice for yourself. Add your current *SKILL*. This total is **your** Attack Strength.

3. Whose Attack Strength is higher? If your Attack Strength is higher, you have wounded the creature. If the creature's Attack Strength is higher, it has wounded you. (If both are the same, you have both missed – start

the next Attack Round from step 1 above.)

4. If you wounded the creature, subtract 2 points from its *STAMINA* score. You may use *LUCK* here to do additional damage (see "Using Luck in Battles" below).

5. If the creature wounded you, subtract 2 points from your *STAMINA* score. You may use *LUCK* to minimize the damage (see below).

6. Make the appropriate changes to either the creature's or your own *STAMINA* scores (and your *LUCK* score if you used *LUCK*) and begin the next Attack Round (repeat steps 1–6).

7. This continues until the *STAMINA* score of either you or the creature you are fighting has been reduced to zero (death).

ESCAPING FROM BATTLES

On some pages you will be given the option of Escaping from the battle. You may only Escape if it is offered to you on the page. If you do run away, the creature automatically scores one wound on you (subtract 2

STAMINA points) as you flee. Such is the price of cowardice. You can use LUCK on this wound in the normal way (see 'Using Luck in Battles' below).

LUCK

Sometimes you will be told to *Test Your Luck*. As you will discover, using *LUCK* is a risky business. The way you *Test Your Luck* is as follows:

Roll two dice. If the number rolled is equal to or less than your current *LUCK* score, you have been *Lucky*. If the number rolled is higher than your current *LUCK* score, you have been *Unlucky*. The consequences of being *Lucky* or *Unlucky* will be found on the page. Each time you *Test Your Luck,* you must subtract one point from your current *LUCK* score. So the more you rely on luck, the more risky this becomes.

USING LUCK IN BATTLES

In battles, you always have the option of using your *LUCK* either to score a more serious wound on a creature, or to minimize the effects of a wound the creature has just scored on you.

IF YOU HAVE JUST WOUNDED THE CREATURE: you may *Test Your Luck* as described below. If you are *Lucky*, subtract an extra 2 points from the creature's *STAMINA* score (i.e., 4 instead of 2 normally). But if you are *Unlucky*, you must restore 1 point to the creature's *STAMINA* (so instead of scoring the normal 2 points of damage, you have now only scored 1).

IF THE CREATURE HAS JUST WOUNDED YOU: you can *Test Your Luck* to try to minimize the wound. If you are lucky, restore 1 point of your *STAMINA* (i.e., instead of doing 2 points of damage, it has done only 1). If you are unlucky, subtract 1 extra *STAMINA* point.

Don't forget to subtract 1 point from your *LUCK* score each time you *Test Your Luck*.

RESTORING SKILL, STAMINA AND LUCK

Occasionally, a page may give instructions to alter your skill score. A Magic Weapon may increase your *SKILL*, but remember that only one weapon can be used at a time! You cannot claim 2 *SKILL* bonuses for carrying two Magic Swords. Your *SKILL* score can never exceed its *initial* value unless specifically instructed. You may only restore your SKILL score by using a Skill Spell (see USING MAGIC).

STAMINA AND PROVISIONS

Your *STAMINA* score will change a lot during the adventure. As you near your goal, your *STAMINA* level may become dangerously low and battles may be particularly risky, so be careful!

You may only restore your STAMINA score by casting a Stamina Spell (see USING MAGIC). You are well advised to ensure that you include Stamina Spells in your original choice of spells. Remember also that your STAMINA score may never exceed its initial value.

LUCK

You will find additions to your *LUCK* score awarded when you have been particularly *Lucky*. Remember that, as with *SKILL* and *STAMINA*, your *LUCK* score may never exceed its *initial* value unless specifically instructed on a page. You may otherwise only restore your LUCK score by using a Luck Spell (see USING MAGIC).

EQUIPMENT AND POTIONS

In addition to SKILL, STAMINA and LUCK scores, you must also determine your MAGIC score in a similar way.

Roll two dice. Add 6 to the number rolled and enter this total in the MAGIC box on your Adventure Sheet.

Your MAGIC score determines how many Magic Spells you may use during your quest. These spells may be chosen from the list following this section. After considering the spells available, enter your choices in the Magic Spells box on your Adventure Sheet.

If, for example, you roll a 4 and a 3, your MAGIC score will be 13 (i.e. 4+3+6), which means you will be able to use thirteen spells on your adventure. From the list of spells over the next page, you may choose thirteen spells as you please. Perhaps you would like to take three Stamina Spells, five E.S.P Spells and five Fire Spells – or maybe you prefer one of each of the twelve spells plus an extra Creature Copy Spell. The choice is yours.

Each time, during the adventure, that you use a spell, you must cross it off your list (even if it is not effective).

If you have taken more than one of any spell, you must reduce the number available by one each time you use it. You will sometimes be given the option to use spells and find that you have not got them with you, or have used them all up. In these cases, you may not choose these options.

As you will have no idea of the dangers lurking within the Citadel the first time you enter, you will no doubt choose spells which will not be as effective as you would like. But on subsequent adventures, you will choose your spells more wisely. Also, don't worry if your MAGIC score is low. Even the lowest possible score will provide you with enough spells to complete your quest if you make the right choices and are blessed with a little luck!

MAGIC SPELLS

CREATURE COPY

This spell will allow you to conjure up an exact duplicate of any creature you are fighting. The duplicate will have the same SKILL and STAMINA scores, and the same powers, as its original. But the duplicate will be under the control of your will and you may, for example, instruct it to attack the original creature and then sit back and watch the battle!

E.S.P.

With this spell you will be able to tune in to psychic wavelengths. It may help you to read a creature's mind or may tell you what is behind a locked door. However, it is sometimes prone to give misleading information if one psychic source is close to another.

FIRE

Every creature is afraid of fire, and this spell allows you to conjure up fire at will. You may cause a small explosion on the ground which will burn for several seconds or you may create a wall of fire to keep creatures at bay.

FOOL'S GOLD

This spell will turn ordinary rock into a pile of what appears to be gold. However, the spell is merely a form of illusion spell – although more reliable than the Illusion Spell below – and the pile of gold will soon turn back to rock.

ILLUSION

This is a powerful spell, but one which is a little unreliable. Through this spell you may create a convincing illusion (e.g. that you have turned into a snake, or that the floor is covered in hot coals) with which to fool a creature. The spell will immediately be cancelled if anything happens which dispels the illusion (e.g. you convince a creature that you have turned into a snake and then promptly crack it over the head with your sword!). It is most effective against intelligent creatures.

LEVITATION

You may cast this spell onto objects, opponents and even

yourself. It frees its receiver from the effects of gravity and as such will cause that receiver to float freely in the air, under your control.

LUCK

This spell, along with the Skill and Stamina spells, is special in that it may be cast at any time during your adventure, except in battle. You need not wait for a choice to appear on the page. Once cast, it will restore your LUCK score by half your initial Luck score (if your initial LUCK score is an odd number, deduct the extra ½). This spell will never take your LUCK score over its initial level. Thus if you cast two Luck Spells together, your LUCK score will only be restored to its initial level.

SHIELDING

Casting this spell creates an invisible shield in front of you which will protect you from physical objects, e.g. arrows, swords or creatures. The shield is not effective against magic and, of course, if nothing outside can touch you, you will not be able to touch anything outside it.

SKILL

This spell will replenish your STAMINA score by half its initial value and may be cast at any time, except in battle. See the Luck Spell for rules.

STRENGTH

This spell has the effect of increasing your strength greatly and is very useful when battling strong creatures. However, it must be exercised with caution as it is difficult to control your own strength when it is suddenly increased by so much!

WEAKNESS

Strong creatures are reduced by this spell to miserable weaklings. It is not successful against all creatures but when effective, those creatures become puny and much less of a challenge in a battle.

EQUIPMENT

You start your adventure with a sword and dressed in leather armour. You carry a lantern to light your way, and a backpack to hold any treasure or artefacts you may find on your way. Be sure to record all your finds in your Equipment box on your Adventure Sheet. When these are used in any particular encounter, the story will tell you whether that item is destroyed or left behind. If it is lost in this way, you must cross it off your list of Equipment and you may not use it later in the adventure.

HINTS ON PLAY

It will probably take you several attempts to make your way through *The Citadel of Chaos*. Make notes and draw a map as you explore – this map will be useful in future adventures and help you identify unexplored areas.

Not all locations contain treasure; many merely contain traps and creatures. There are many "wild-goose chase" passages, and while you may progress through to your ultimate destination, it is by no means certain that you will win.

May the luck of the gods go with you on the adventure ahead!

ADVENTURE SHEET

SKILL ☐

STAMINA ☐

LUCK ☐

EQUIPMENT

GOLD

MAGIC ☐

MAGIC SPELLS

MONSTER ENCOUNTERS

MONSTER:
SKILL =
STAMINA =

MONSTER:
SKILL =
STAMINA =

MONSTER:
SKILL =
STAMINA =

MONSTER:
SKILL =
STAMINA =

MONSTER:
SKILL =
STAMINA =

MONSTER:
SKILL =
STAMINA =

MONSTER:
SKILL =
STAMINA =

MONSTER:
SKILL =
STAMINA =

MONSTER:
SKILL =
STAMINA =

MONSTER:
SKILL =
STAMINA =

MONSTER:
SKILL =
STAMINA =

MONSTER:
SKILL =
STAMINA =